PRINCE, POPE VAMPIRE

David Herder

Amazon

CONTENTS

INTRODUCTION

Dear Dave,

My time here has ended and I must move on. This has happened often, for a very long time. It is not vanity for me to say that I am older than I look.

The enclosed flash drive contains that portion of my memories relevant to my purposes. They, and any profit you may derive from them are yours. In fact, you should claim authorship because no one will believe that I exist.

This expresses my appreciation for your knowing who Pope John XII was and particularly for something you said a couple of years ago. A few of us were sitting around and the topic of the pedophile scandals in the Catholic Church came up. As such conversations do, the topic meandered a bit and a Jesuit-educated man said that the worst pope in history was a thousand years ago whose name was John but he could not remember the number, a man on the order of Caligula. You said that was probably John XII and—what I really appreciated—that you had some sympathy for him. "He was a kid of 18 whose father, to secure dynastic advantages, had forced him into the priesthood and then arranged to have him elected pope." The reasons for my appreciation will become apparent when you read what I have given you.

Vampire stories have become a current fad. You said that you never saw or read any of the *Twilight* books or movies because "a sweet, love-stricken puppy does not make a creditable vampire." Talking about vampire movies in general, you commented that in all of them the vampire was already well-established and wondered how someone is chosen to become a vampire and how he knew that he was a vampire and how to be one. That led me to think about telling the true story of a vampire. How I know will also become apparent.

Goodbye and best wishes,
Sebastian Smith

PROLOGUE

Can Sebastian's story be true? The first reaction is "Of course not!" When I received the manuscript I checked various sources and found his descriptions of events and personalities accurate; of course, the same sources were available to him.

Sebastian Smith was about average height, perhaps 5' 10" (1.72 meters). Having once been with him when he bought a suit, I know he took a size 41 with a 31-inch waist and 31-inch inseam. I would guess that he weighed 150 – 160 pounds. His face was more square than round, with a medium-sized nose and strong chin. He had ash-blond hair and blue eyes. He looked to be around 25.

We met in the fall of 2009. The day after he moved into a house a couple of doors down from me I was walking past his place as he came out. We exchanged pleasantries and I offered to show him around the neighborhood. As we walked, he said that he worked from home as a consultant on "fluid systems." Having no idea what that was, except that it sounded very technical, I did not pursue it. We became something between acquaintances and friends, seeing each other occasionally. We had a mutual interest in history, movies, and theater and he impressed me as being very well read for so young a man.

There was absolutely no sign that Sebastian was a vampire. But then, I wasn't looking for a sign. Why waste time looking for something that does not exist?

dh

PRINCE AND POPE

A typical representative of the House of Theophylact, concerned with power and sexual liaisons. (Walter Ullmann)

1

Here begins my story which may well be, in every sense, the damnedest thing you have ever heard.

I, Octavian of the House of Theophylact, was born in Rome on the fifth of September in the year of our Lord 937. My father, Alberic II, Count of Tusculum was Patrician and effective ruler of Rome and its environs, and styled himself "Prince of Rome." My mother, Alda, was the daughter of Hugh, King of Italy—though his hold on that title was tenuous and constantly challenged. My mother was a sixth generation descendant of Charlemagne. I was born with every advantage at the apex of Roman society. There were later charges that I was illegitimate, the son of one of my father's mistresses from before his marriage. Not true. A tale spread by my enemies. I am not paranoid, but I did have enemies, as anyone who is born or rises to a high place will have. More on these later.

Erase any picture you may have of Rome as it appeared at the height of the Empire, a vast city of more than 1,000,000 souls. In the tenth century, Rome was a decayed, squalid town of no more than 30,000 inhabitants. The Glory of Rome was present only in the majestic rubble left strewn about the city after centuries of war, looting, and neglect.

Augustus, after whom in hope or whimsy I was named, would have wept to see the wraith of the city that he boasted he "found of brick and left of marble."

The regard in which Rome was held is thus: When our father died, my older brother Gregory received the greater title and richer lands of Count of Tusculum and I was left as Prince of Rome. Gregory commented that the legacy was split because our father doubted that either of us was able to manage the whole. He was probably right.

All families exaggerate their antiquity and the prestige of their forebears. Mine was no exception. The Theophylacts, of Greek origin, had come to Rome several generations previously, when it was part of what is now called the Byzantine Empire but to its last day in 1453 called itself the Roman Empire. We believed that a Theophylact had been sent by the great Justinian himself in an official capacity around 540. Of this there is no evidence whatsoever. Some 200 years before my birth a Theophylact was named Exarch of Ravenna by Emperor Justinian II. The Exarch was governor of the Italian possessions of the Emperor. We claimed him as one of us. However and whenever we arrived, the family had over the decades, perhaps centuries, increased its estates and wealth. By the beginning of the 10th century, the town of Tusculum in the Alban Hills, about 25 kilometers (16 miles) southeast of Rome, was ruled by my great-grandfather, Theophylact I, the first of the family for whom there is solid documentary evidence. He married the redoubtable Theodora, Senatrix of Rome, considered by all the dominant partner in the marriage.

The family's greatness, if it may be so characterized, began with Theodora's daughter, the even more redoubtable Marozia, my grandmother. She was the mistress of one pope (Sergius III), perhaps a second (John X), mother of another (John XI, by Sergius), grandmother of two (John XII, your humble chronicler, and Benedict VII) and, finally, great-grandmother of three (Benedict VIII, John XIX and Benedict IX). The seven of us reigned, interspersed among others, from 904 to 1047. Several of those "interspersed" represented the Crescenti family, who were both our cousins (through Theodora the Younger, sister to Marozia) and bitterest enemies. Theodora the Younger's grandson, John Crescentius, my second cousin, became my second successor, after the one year pontificate of Leo VIII, as John XIII.

During this period, the so-called *saeculum obscurum* (dark age), the selection of a Pope was no stately conclave ending with a puff of smoke. The Papacy was controlled by whichever Roman family or outside faction had the power to seize it, often ending with blood in the streets. By way of explanation, the term "dark age" is used to denote the nadir of the Papacy, not the dearth of learning, though there was not much of that either. An even less kindly term for the era is the *Pornocracy* (government by harlots) because of the way Marozia and both Theodoras pursued their objectives.

Marozia was married three times. First to my grandfather Alberic I, named Patrician of Rome upon the marriage and later succeeded his father-in-law as Count of Tusculum. This Alberic had started as a page to Guy III, Duke of Spoleto, and rose in prominence and power until, just before the year 900 he murdered Guy IV and became Duke. This was a not uncommon method of advancement. He was legitimated as Duke by the King of Italy, Berengar I, a close ally. The height of his power came at Battle of the Garigliano (915) a short way north of Rome, where the Saracens had taken and fortified a town from which to threaten central Italy. Pope John X personally led the Christian forces drawn from Italy and the Byzantine territory around Bari. Alberic commanded the troops of Berengar, who did not participate. This was all to the good since it has been recorded that in 40 years of campaigning, Berengar never won a battle. With overwhelming forces, the Christians won an overwhelming victory, virtually exterminating the Saracens. They were the last infidels to invade Italy in my lifetime though, as will unfold hereafter, the same cannot be said of my fellow Christians.

After the battle, Alberic I was named Consul of Rome and became the nominal ruler of the city. He was not, however, an effective ruler, becoming increasingly despotic and ruling through barbarian mercenaries. About 918 the Pope, still John

X, and despite his purported affair with Marozia, combined with the Roman nobility to drive Alberic out of Rome. It can be assumed that Alberic retreated to his father-in-law's lands in Tusculum, which he inherited upon the death of Theophylact I in 924, only to be murdered a few months later.

As my father was only 12, Marozia became regent and the *de facto* ruler of Tusculum. Within a year of my grandfather's death, she married Guy, Margrave of Tuscany.

She now took her revenge on John X. Uniting her forces with those of Guy, she attacked Rome, seized John and imprisoned him in the Crescenti fortress (now the Castel Sant'Angelo) where he soon died, either through starvation or being smothered by a pillow.

Guy died shortly thereafter (929) and Marozia set her sights on the married Hugh of Arles, King of Italy and half-brother to Guy. Marozia's control of Rome, Tusculum and the Papacy made her, though now 40, a highly desirable match. Marozia and Hugh were within the Canon Law definition of consanguinity and prohibited from marrying. Hugh had his mother's second marriage declared invalid, legally bastardizing Guy and his family but removing that impediment to the marriage.

Alberic was now 20 and it was whispered to him that Hugh and Marozia were going to blind him to take control of his patrimony. He was able to put together a conspiracy consisting of the Roman nobility who wanted to maintain Rome's independence and Hugh and Marozia's enemies—a sizable group. In December 932, during the wedding celebration Alberic and Hugh came to blows, Alberic stormed out and returned a short time later with his soldiers and a mob of Romans he had persuaded to follow him. Hugh escaped by jumping through a window but Marozia was captured and spent the rest of her life as her son's prisoner.

Mere hatred cannot be allowed to interfere with the necessities of statecraft. Thus, early in 936 Alberic was married to Hugh's daughter Alda, who was also, if you have been paying attention, his stepsister and later that year my brother Gregory was born, named after the Pope. The next year was graced with my birth and, as we have seen, named after Octavian Augustus, the first Roman Emperor, which speaks loudly of my father's ambitions.

As a ruler, Alberic II was the most competent of the Theophylacts—not, admittedly, a difficult standard to reach. He managed to dominate the nobles of Rome and Tusculum, always prickly in guarding what they considered their prerogatives, as well as keeping the lower orders peaceful through an effective blending of food and fear.

I was given an excellent education—the trivium (grammar, logic, rhetoric) and the quadrivium (arithmetic, geometry, music, astronomy). Instruction was in both Latin and Greek; I also picked up the Roman dialect, mostly from street companions considered "beneath your station."

Also, of course, training in arms. The Law was what the strongest said it was. Whatever one possessed had to be defended, whatever one wanted had to be seized. Those who could, like my father, organized their own force. The weaker would align themselves with men, again like my father, who could offer protection. I took to soldiering. The hours spent in training were among the most enjoyable of my childhood.

Gregory was the "good boy," conscientious, obedient, moral, possessed of all the virtues that make men detested. I suspect he was chaste until his wedding night. We were brothers, but not friends. To my surprise, the smug prig became an effective ruler and some years after the end of my reign became Duke of Rome, thus effectively reuniting our father's domains and he lived until 1012. I shall say in his favor that during my travails he would, from time to time, assist me.

2

At the age of 14 my hormones kicked in with a vengeance. I went to bed anticipating the erotic dreams, which came almost every night, sometimes twice, that I found both satisfying for the pleasure and frustrating that they were not the real experience. Shortly before my fifteenth birthday my father sent me with some documents to Aurelian Severus, one of his lieutenants who lived five or six houses from us on the Via Lata, toward the Campus Martius, telling me to wait if he were not home. Wealthy and eccentric, the Severi lived as if they were in Augustus' Rome. When I pulled the bell cord, the door was opened by a female slave. Upon asking for Aurelian Severus, she said he was not in, would I care to see the mistress? Since I knew them both from visits to my father's house, I thought I could leave the documents with her. I was seated in the anteroom while the slave went to get Faustina. When she came in, I gasped. I had only seen her in a stola, a capacious, enclosing garment. At home, she was wearing a tunic which showed her beautiful legs and very appealing figure.

"My...my father wants me to give these to your husband. Will he be home soon?"

"No. He is seeing to some business, but will return this evening. You are welcome to wait."

She came closer, pointed to my crotch, smiled broadly and said, "That is very flattering." I was aware of my erection but was surprised at how obvious it was. I felt myself flush but did have the presence of mind to say, "You are very beautiful." I began to sweat.

Now we were so close that we were almost touching. She took a handkerchief and wiped my forehead. "And you are quite the handsome young man." I was having trouble breathing.

She put her arms around me, put her hands on my buttocks, and did a sort of massage. I did the same for her, partly to have something to hang on to—my knees were shaking, my heart was pounding and I was as excited and happy as I could remember ever being.

"You are trembling. There's nothing to be afraid of.

"It's not fear." I could get my voice barely above a whisper.

Still smiling she said, "I really did not think that it was. Come with me. I want to show you a few things." She took my hand and brought me upstairs and opened a door to a room without windows, but the ceiling had several circular glass skylights, perhaps fifteen to eighteen inches in diameter which, on a sunny day like this lit the room brightly. The walls were painted with men and women from almost naked to entirely naked, engaged in various erotic activities that that would fit most people's definition of pornography. There were even some animals joining into the revels. Laughing, Faustina put a hand gently under my chin to close my gaping mouth. I began to understand what "Roman orgy" meant.

The room had a large, comfortable bed to which she led me. Even at that age, I was not so innocent as not to know what was about to happen. It did. True to her promise, Faustina showed me things other than the paintings. Foremost, that sex was meant for two and with future experiments I preferred it with women.

After we finished, Faustina said that Aurelian Severus would be returning soon and I waited while we had cider and cake. He came in at dusk, I gave him the documents, thanked Faustina yet again and went home.

Upon entering the house, I was told to go to my father.

"Aurelian Severus was out and I had to wait."

"I hope the time past pleasantly."

"Oh, yes. Faustina was most gracious."

He gave a little laugh, "I have always found that to be true. By the way, do not tell your mother you spent the afternoon with Faustina, they do not really like each other."

I started to ask why, but he said, "Thank you. You can go now, I'm busy."

Later, before dinner, I saw Gregory who told me, "Father let me attend an interesting meeting about making the water in Rome cleaner, the whole council was here and I got to sit in. If you took more interest in the government, he might let you attend." The smug ass thought he was scoring one off me, but what caught my attention was that Aurelian Severus was on the council.

I had now discovered sex and fallen in love, not with anyone in particular, anyway after my puppy love for Faustina passed, but with sex itself. In my position, women were easy, offering themselves, not, as I naively believed, because of my irresistible appeal but in hope of a piece of silver or a favor from my father. Their men were even worse, willing to send wives and daughters to my room for the same reasons. One of my friends even mentioned his mother in the hope that "you will remember me when you are our ruler." I reveled in it, taking every advantage that fate had given me. My mother would remind me of my "station" and not to become too familiar with the "lower orders." They would not respect what they knew too well. My father, whose own morals were no more exemplary than mine, was more indulgent.

3

At 16, I had a surprise from my father. He had decided that, to consolidate the family's hold on Rome, I should be the next Pope. Therefore, I was to take Holy Orders. When he told me,

I laughed, pointing out that "the words holy and Octavian have not been used together since my baptism."

"That is irrelevant. Having the Papacy will strengthen your hold on the government. The common people are in awe of the office and it can be used as a counterweight to the nobles, who will always try to claw away at your authority."

"I can't live like that! I won't! I go to bed every night with a woman and wake up in the morning looking for another."

"That does not have to change. Almost every Pope of my lifetime has had the morals of a tom cat. You will have to exercise more circumspection and seek out a better class of women."

"Why? The peasants are happy with a few coins and actually seek me out. The 'better class,' as you call them don't want money, they want me to coax a favor from you."

"My point exactly. As Pope you will be in the powerful position of being able to grant or withhold favors—contracts, appointments, lands, and... oh, almost any of their wishes. As long as they think their interests coincide with yours, rather than another's, they will remain loyal—in their fashion."

"What will God think? The church can do better."

"Better than what? Better than the pious old fool who is pope now?"

"Agepetus is much loved by the people and he contents himself exclusively with the Church, allowing you full control of the politics of Rome."

"Yes, but you cannot count on such deference. There are many in the Church who use the Donation of Pepin to hold a much exaggerated idea of the temporal power of the Pope over Rome and, indeed, all of central Italy as far as Ravenna. They think that I am usurping Papal lands and authority. In order to assure that Rome stays in the family you need to assume the

Papacy."

At this point, I should remind you that marriage, while discouraged, was not forbidden to the clergy in the 10th century. The movement toward celibacy was gaining currency but did not become rigorously enforced until the reforms of Gregory VII at the end of the 11th century. My father, who thought in epic terms, was assuming that I would pass Rome, and perhaps even the chair of St. Peter to my and his descendants.

And so it was that I was ordained in the spring of 954, aged not yet 17. Soon after, my childhood ended. My father took ill and, when it became clear that he would not recover, induced the nobility of Rome to promise that I would be the next Pope. His Chamberlain, Julius, and I were given the inducements—money, lands, and titles--to be paid upon my election. Satisfied with his arrangements, Alberic II died after 22 years of rule at the age of 42. Living much beyond that was the exception among the swamps and fevers of Rome.

4

Prince of Rome at 17: I had a core of support from my father's closest allies among the nobility of Rome. They were generally the lesser nobles who did not have the power to aspire to my position and had looked for protection from the predations of their more powerful neighbors by aligning with us. My father had been very adept at keeping this group satisfied while managing the rivalries of those who aspired to replace him so that there was never a combination to mount a serious challenge to him. I was not at all certain that I was equally deft.

It must be admitted that being Prince did not seriously crimp my pleasures. My father had left much good will and a full treasury. This enabled public spectacles, as when I assumed my diocese as Cardinal and deacon of the church of Santa Maria in Domnica, as well as more personal expenses. Julius, about 15 years older than I, was invaluable, keeping everything running smoothly and, except for occasional carping about my spending, largely leaving me alone. He was the perfect servant. A poor boy who began working in our fields at 7 or 8, he had impressed my father with his quick tongue when mocked by his "betters." He had been taken in and educated by my father and was totally loyal. He had no connections with the nobility, indeed they envied him and thought he had "risen above his station." The nobility assured his loyalty by snubbing him. He knew that his power would not outlast mine.

A little over a year after my father's death, Pope Agepetus II died at what was then a very advanced age, probably nearing 60.

5

Pope John XII

Everything went according to my father's script, and I was elected Pope on December 16, 955. I was only the third Pope not to use his own name; after all, I was named after a Roman emperor. The first to do so was John II whose given name was Mercurius. He felt that bearing the name of a Roman God would not adequately convey the mission of the Papacy. I became, in essence, two persons: for all affairs of the Church, I was Pope John XII; for all secular business, I remained Prince Octavian.

For about two years, the system my father had put in place held fairly well. For the Church, I found an intelligent, low-born priest, Bartholomew, to act as what would now be called my administrative assistant. He kept the paper work flowing, and there was a lot of it. Even though the Papacy did not have the overwhelming authority over the Church that it later acquired, all manner of things, particularly disputes between or within dioceses were referred to Rome for adjudication. I was reasonably conscientious in reviewing the more difficult matters, leaving Bartholomew to handle the routine. While the Pope did not yet have the power to name bishops—that generally resided with the temporal rulers—he did need to bestow the pallium upon new bishops. Given the speed of communications, by the time the bishop's name got to me, he had often been in office for several months. I would always adjure them to lead a good and holy life. Do not mock. As Pope, I was pure; all my sins were secular.

Then came confusion in the English Church. Oda, Archbishop of Canterbury died in mid-958 and King Eadwig nominated the Bishop of Winchester, Ælfsige, to succeed him. Passing through the Alps on his way to Rome to receive the pallium, he encountered a severe winter storm and perished in the cold. Eadwig next nominated Byrhthelm, Bishop of Wells. Before Byrhthelm could leave England, Eadwig died and his successor, his brother Edgar, withdrew the nomination on the grounds that Byrhthelm had not been able to govern the Diocese of Wells competently. Edgar's choice was Dunstan, Bishop of Worcester and London. As Pope I had to resolve between the claimants. Not that I hesitated. When I bestowed the pallium on Dustan, the most important see in a very important country had been vacant for two years. The wait proved worthwhile in every respect. St. Dunstan, as he became shortly after his death, was the saintliest man I ever met and proved one of the great Archbishops of Canterbury, a towering figure in the medieval Church. Let it be noted that I did give some good service to the Church.

All this time, however, I was concentrating on the secular side of my responsibilities. Over the previous few years, the duchies of Capua and Benevento, to the south and east of Rome, had been encroaching on Papal lands and I had been raising an army to reclaim them. Pulling together forces from all the family dominions—Rome, Tusculum, Spoleto—I marched south in the spring of 960. The size of the papal army caused the dukes to go running to Gisulf, Prince of Salerno who sent his army, threatening to get behind mine, which would have pinned me between my foes. I retreated to Rome, simultaneously sending Julius to Gisulf to try to detach him from the alliance. As he often did, Julius succeeded. At the price of releasing Salerno from being a Papal fiefdom, which in any event I could not enforce, Gisulf abandoned his partners. Having now been maintaining an army in the field for almost two months, the strain on the treasury was becoming critical. Small adjustments to the borders and the dukes saying in effect, "Oops, we didn't know this was yours," allowed both side to claim victory and salvage their dignity.

I returned to Rome to find that a powerful faction of the nobility was plotting to usurp my temporal power. To this end, they had called upon the King of Italy, Berengar II, grandson of the Berengar who was my grandfather's ally. This both suited Berengar and demonstrated the political naiveté of my opponents—Berengar's goal was nothing less than to incorporate the States of the Church into his own domains. This Berengar had been forced to submit to King Otto I of Germany in 952, whose vassal he then became.

A residual effect of Charlemagne's empire was that northern Italy was considered part of Germany. The King of Germany was an elective position, though Otto succeeded his father, and ruled through his major vassals, the great dukes, counts and minor kings, like Berengar.

Within a few years, however, Otto's strongest generals in Italy, his brother Henry, Duke of Bavaria, and son Liudolf, Duke of Swabia, had died, leaving a power vacuum as Otto himself was in Germany. Berengar II exploited this vacuum and encroached upon Otto's territories in Italy.

You have noticed the number of deaths. Life was uncertain and while the wealthy had a longer expectancy than the poor, it was still not much beyond fifty and often younger. Henry was in his mid-30's and Liudolf 27. Though Otto I made it to 60, neither of his successors, his son and grandson, both also named Otto, reached 30 and the death of Otto III at 21 ended the dynasty. All died of "fever," which covered anything the limited medical knowledge of the day could not otherwise identify.

At this time, 960, Otto was the most powerful man in Europe. King of Germany and Duke of Saxony since the age of 24 in 936, he had won the greatest military victory of the century at the Battle of Lechfeld, just outside of Augsburg, Bavaria in 955 over the invading Hungarians. Though greatly outnumbered—some accounts have it at two to one—the Germans were made up of armored knights and heavily armed infantry while the Hungarians were shooting arrows from their smaller horses. The survivors of the Hungarian forces fled back to Hungary, never again to come westward. The Germans, themselves exhausted, could not pursue them. Thus Otto earned the epithet "the Great," bestowed by history upon those who successfully steal a great deal of land from their neighbors.

I, along with several other threatened rulers, had sent ambassadors to Otto asking for help against Berengar. This was the autumn of 960. At medieval speed, Otto arrived in Italy with his army in August, 961. Being no match for the King's forces, Berengar abandoned his conquests and retreated to his strongholds. Otto deposed him and assumed the title of King of Italy. Tidying up as he moved south, Otto reached Rome at the end of January, 962. In the negotiations for Otto's help, he had stipulated that he be crowned Roman Emperor, emulating Charlemagne. The title had not been used since the death of Berengar I in 924, but then survived until 1806. Otto is generally held to be the first Holy Roman Emperor though that name did not come into use for another 300 years. Not many can say they began an institution that lasted more than 800 years. On February 2, 962 in a great and solemn ceremony at St. Peter's, I anointed Otto and his wife, Adelaide, as Emperor and Empress of the Romans. I must say that Otto, at nearly 50, whatever his faults, and they were many, looked like an emperor. Taller than average for that time and ramrod straight, with a strong, rectangular clean-shaven face and thick, curly brown hair falling to his shoulders and covering his ears. I never discovered whether the curls were nature or art.

Adelaide was the first to be anointed Empress, a richly deserved honor. Married at 15 to the King of Italy, Lothair II, she bore him a daughter before he was murdered by his successor, the same Berengar we were now fighting. Upon her refusal to marry his son, Adalbert, Berengar imprisoned her. She escaped a few months later and after some trials and danger, arrived at Otto's court to plead for protection. Otto was so impressed with this woman of courage, intelligence, station, and beauty that he married her. After Otto's death, in 973, she entered a convent, emerging in 991 to act as Regent for her grandson, Otto III, until he came of age in 995. She died toward the end of 999, confidently awaiting the Second Coming upon the millennium. For her works of charity, she was canonized in 1097. Altogether, one of the most impressive people I have ever met. Had Otto possessed her character he would truly have earned his epithet.

The historically unfortunate result of the Holy Roman Empire is that it probably prevented the unification of Germany in step with other feudal entities like France, on its west and Poland and Russia to the east. The ablest and strongest emperors after Otto, the Hohenstaufen (1138 – 1268) spent their time and strength chasing the chimera of retaining Italy in the empire which forced them to give powers and privileges to their German vassals. When, at last, the Italian dream vanished, the vassals and, more importantly, the empire's neighbors were in a position to create coalitions to block all attempts of the later, weakened emperors to centralize the empire.

Back to our story. The evening of the coronation, I held a banquet for the new Emperor and Empress, their retinue, the nobility of Rome, and other notables who had come to Rome to participate or just to watch the festivities. The Papal huntsmen provided venison, boar, small game and fowls. In the dead of winter the vegetables were carrots, turnips, cabbage, barley, lentil and other beans. Copious amounts of wine, beer and cider were consumed, several of the revelers dropping off before we finally dragged ourselves to bed as dawn was breaking. There was music and dancing, jesters and jugglers, and a very impressive magician. Everyone was gracious enough to say what a wonderful time they were having. Our cooks surpassed themselves. I remember the food as being the best I ever had. However, as hard as I try, I cannot recall how anything tasted.

The next day we began negotiations and, as his part of the bargain, Otto and I signed a treaty recognizing the Pope as the secular ruler of the States of the Church, extending the territory to Ravenna, Spoleto, and several other fiefs. I secured with a legitimate piece of paper that which the Church had only claimed through the forgery, The Donation of Constantine. Otto also committed the Emperor to protecting the Church and its lands. It quickly became apparent that Otto had no intention of observing the Treaty. He did not cede the territories promised, among many other broken promises.

The treaty stipulated that the clergy and people of Rome would elect the Pope; the Pope, however, was required to swear an oath of allegiance to the Emperor.

It soon became evident that Otto was intent on restricting the Papacy only to ecclesiastical duties. He would take care of secular affairs. He was the first that I know of who claimed that because God put him on the throne, he had a "divine right" to rule and answered to none but God. That idea persisted, with weakening force, as long as the Holy Roman Empire.

The cities within the States of the Church were required swear loyalty to the Emperor rather than the Pope. This would essentially strip my authority both as Pope over the States of the Church and my hereditary powers as Prince of Rome. Seeking to protect both the Church and myself, I entered into negotiations with my enemy's enemy, Berengar's son, Adalbert, and through him with Berengar himself. I also sent ambassadors to the Byzantines and Magyars in an attempt to form a coalition against Otto, now feared by everyone. I have been much reviled for this as I had taken an oath on the bones of St. Peter not to aid Berengar and Adalbert. In return, Otto had pledged the independence of the States of the Church and the secular authority of the Pope. His perfidy released me from my oath. As the cliché has it, history is written by the victors; in this case the historian was Luidprand of Cremona, an apologist for Otto.

My ambassadors were captured by Otto's men and "persuaded" to reveal their mission and that Adalbert was in Rome with me. Otto quickly seized and imprisoned Berengar and moved towards Rome. Striving to resolve the conflict and persuade the Emperor to keep his side of the treaty I sent ambassadors to Otto. One of the party was Leo, superintendent of the public schools of Rome, a layman of whom more shortly.

Otto did not stop. As his advance guard attempted to cross the Tiber, I donned full armor and led my army against them. We met them outside the city walls as they were coming out of the river. They had a small advantage in cavalry but the ground was semi-swamp and I ordered our cavalry to dismount and throw weighted ropes around the legs of the struggling horses, killing the fallen riders with axe and pike. Our infantry was meanwhile engaged in heavy fighting so I ran to help and saw a soldier with sword and buckler running toward me. It was the first time I was fighting for my life but one has no time to think of anything except surviving the fight. I stopped and braced myself and his momentum carried him into me. As he swung his sword I was able to deflect it with my buckler and it glanced harmlessly off my well-armored shoulder. The gesture left him open and I thrust my sword into his mid-section, piercing the leather corselet. Dropping his sword, he grasped my right arm just above the haft of my sword and I grabbed his left arm with my left hand. Our faces were only inches apart and his expression was more of surprise than fear. He made no sound. I felt him tremble and then he fell against me. I let him slide to the ground, pulling out my sword. My first kill. I was a soldier. The fight lasted only seconds but it seems longer in my memory. I turned toward the fighting but the Papal army was driving the imperial troops back across the river.

At the same time a coordinated uprising by my enemies, and Otto's friends, within Rome had succeeded in occupying a fortified section of the city. This was the beginning of a long battle within Rome between the imperial party and the nationalists who wanted to preserve the independence of Rome. Being informed of the uprising, Julius gathered the few remaining Papal guards and attacked. He sent a messenger and I rode with a contingent of soldiers to his aid. Upon seeing us, the rebels retreated into their stronghold. In his haste, Julius had not put on armor, only grabbing a sword and buckler. I found his body, covered with blood, his tunic ripped with several wounds. I fell to my knees, cradled him and wept. Julius was my best friend and right arm. The captain of the guard put his hands on my shoulders and gently tried to lift me. "He's safe now." I rose, barely seeing through the tears. Someone said, "He died as a man should. There are three dead enemy near him." We carried him back to the palace.

Knowing that I did not have the strength to oppose the entire imperial army, I gathered up loyal forces, the Papal treasury, and withdrew to well-fortified Tivoli, north-east of Rome. Upon entering Rome, Otto called an uncanonical synod that, under threat, deposed me and elected the aforementioned treacherous Leo as the anti-pope Leo VIII. One of Otto's toadies, Sico, Cardinal-Bishop of Ostia, proceeded over a two day period to move Leo through the ranks from layman to acolyte to ordination to deacon to bishop and finally, on December 6, 963, to anti-pope. Such was the worth of Otto's "protection."

In early January Otto released many of his soldiers—who were very expensive to maintain—and returned north, confident of his settlement. My good and faithful Romans had other ideas. They did not accept the sham of Leo's ordination or enthronement under *force majeure* to the Chair of St. Peter. Otto had scarcely left when a revolt broke out, Leo fled to him and I was back by the middle of February. "Leo VIII" had reigned for two months.

Certain bookkeeping chores needed to follow. I called a canonical synod which formally deposed and excommunicated Leo. One would not think it necessary to undo a completely illegal act, but form must be observed.

I was certain that Leo's story would bring Otto back to Rome. Because Otto was still in Italy, it would only take as long as he needed to raise a sufficient force to reconquer Rome. I cast about for allies, of which there were none left in Italy with the will or strength to oppose him. I was becoming desperate at finding no way to preserve Rome and the Papacy.

But it was left to others to face the Emperor.

6

Sex will be the Death of me yet

I was not so desperate as to neglect the pleasures of my current mistress.

I had attempted to make peace with the Crescenti by appointing one of them, Andrew, a grandson of the younger Theodora and thus my second cousin, to a lucrative administrative post. Actually, peace with the Crescenti was only half, maybe less, of my motivation.

Andrew's wife, Agnes, was about my age and very beautiful, of medium height with a soft face tending toward oval, and brown hair and eyes but what I, and most other men noticed first were her breasts, large and firm. I gave Andrew a position that required him to be out of the city often. Agnes was of an old, though relatively impoverished family. She had used her beauty to advance her fortune and Andrew was the one she snared, much to his delight. She was more than willing to have me keep her company when Andrew was away. She liked the money his position generated, allowing her to live in the style to which she felt her lineage entitled her. Sleeping with me was her contribution to the family's prosperity.

Beyond her beauty was her knowledge of how to maximize a man's pleasure. She knew techniques that, even with all my experience, were new to me. I can honestly say that many of the happiest times of my life were in bed with her.

On a fine spring afternoon, we met at one of my small houses, not far from hers. As usual on these occasions I was wearing lay cloths, not the papal cassock, covered by a kind of cloak with a hood that, I hoped, kept me unrecognizable. As usual for these trysts, I had given the servants duties elsewhere so Agnes and I had the place to ourselves. I was first but had just time to shed the cloak when she arrived.

Removing her outer garment revealed a thrilling sight. The dress she was wearing left little to the imagination: thin, almost transparent, making her nipples visible. Also visible, when I finally looked beyond her breasts, was the pubic hair. A most arousing sight and I was aroused. We clinched. I spread my legs so that we could be crotch to crotch, and rubbed our bodies together. One of her hands was down my trousers, the other up my shirt pinching my nipple. My hands were cupping her breasts, the thumbs gently moving back and forth across her nipples. Her dress and my shirt were closed with a row of bows that we began to untie. While engaged thus, we sidled slowly to the bedroom where I pushed her dress off of her shoulders, she doing the same to my shirt while untying my trousers, which fell to the floor. We coated each other with an aromatic oil, claimed to an aphrodisiac—not that I needed one. Agnes had a gift of stretching out the orgasm longer than anyone else I had enjoyed. By the time we reached climax, I was ready to explode.

I took a deep breath and rolled off Agnes onto my back.

There was noise in the next room and, looking through the door, saw Andrew and his page running toward us yelling. I jumped out of bed and, as I tried to fend off the page, Andrew shoved his knife into my abdomen, at the upper edge of the pubic hair. Knowing that if I stopped to lick my wound, I was dead, I grabbed for Andrew's knife with my left hand and despite the pain, swung and caught Andrew's right shoulder with my right elbow which threw him against the bed whence to bounce to the floor, dropping his knife. I lunged at the page who thrust his knife at my midsection, but I was able to parry and knocked him to the floor with a hard punch to the left rib cage. I tried to run but Andrew, still on the floor, grabbed my ankle causing me to fall. Andrew found his knife while still holding my ankle. I twisted onto my back. I kicked at Andrew, halfway up on his knees, who fell forward bringing his knife down as hard as he could. I screamed and thought I would faint from the pain but jerked into a sitting position and swung, hitting Andrew in the jaw. He fell over. I reached for his knife which had pinned my penis and a testicle to the floor. Before I could touch it, the page knelt over me with his knife. I was able to seize his right forearm before the knife came down. I then grabbed his left wrist. Andrew grasped his knife and pulled it toward him, tearing my genitals. Screaming in pain, my grip loosened and the page plunged his knife two inches to the left of my navel. They had me. Andrew stabbed me halfway between the crotch and navel and almost simultaneously the page drove his knife into my left breast, just above the nipple. I was screaming and trying to raise my arms to protect myself but they were too heavy. I could taste blood in my mouth and was becoming dizzy. I saw the both of them bringing their knives down, but everything went black and I did not feel the blades.

All the while Agnes, covering her modesty with the bed-clothes, was screaming "He raped me!" "Don't hurt me!" "Kill him!" in random order.

That last day, May 14, 964 is my most vivid memory. I cling to that memory because it is the last physical sensation I had other than the hunger or relief from the hunger. It is the rec-ollection of the pleasure with Agnes and the pain of the knives which remind me that indeed I once was human.

INTERMEZZO

Just as suddenly everything was light. No colors, no shapes, totally empty, just pure, white light. I had awareness but not substance—consciousness without a body. Was this my soul?

A voice came out of the nothingness, a voice like none I had ever heard—flat, without intonation or timbre, neither male nor female. "Octavian, you have failed in your work."

"Is that why You killed me?" My own voice sounded away, as if I were listening to another person speaking.

"You were entrusted with high positions of the earth and you did not by act or example lift them to a higher plane. Indeed, you degraded almost everything you touched."

"Is that…"

"You will be given an opportunity to speak. Your endeavors as Pope and Prince were aimed solely at indulging your own pleasures and ambitions with no regard of the condition of the people for whom you were responsible. Your life was one of war and fornication. How can you justify your existence?"

"What need have I to justify my existence? I had no choice and was thrown into a life in which everything had already been decided without me. You decreed that I should be Pope and

Prince. Why did you not tell me what you wanted?"

"No one decreed anything. Your life, like all others, was merely the end of random events over infinite time. If any one your ancestors over that infinite time had been different, all subsequent history would have been altered and you never would have been."

Another voice, also without inflection, with just enough variation from the first to tell me it was someone—or something—different. "Is it your intention to give him to me?"

"Yes. He is unworthy." It was the first voice.

"I cannot take him. Do you not hear the prayers for the absolution of his soul?"

It came to me: God and Satan were deciding my fate.

"They are rote, imposed on the monks by Octavian, purchased by gifts and privileges."

Someone was praying for me? Someone able to influence this judgment?

"The prayers are sincere, deeply felt by those pleased to call themselves men of God."

Yes, now I remembered. A few years after becoming Pope I granted a generous charter to the monks of the Abbey of Saint Scholastica, enjoining them to offer frequent, regular masses to almighty God for my salvation. The knowledge that they, at least, had not turned away from me was pleasingly comforting.

The second voice, hereafter Satan, "Nonetheless they bar the way for your servant, John."

The first voice (God), "Servant?! Ha! Everything he ever did was for his own pleasure and advancement. Occasionally, completely accidentally, his action may have served God."

I wondered, would God use the third person? Was I in the presence, without a presence, of the principals or merely representatives? Unless they told me, I should never know.

The two voices were still bickering. God, if that is who it was, said, "It is nothing but simony, trying to buy indulgence instead of earning it, which this sinner never could have done."

"'This sinner' is irrelevant. The virtue of those offering the prayers carries the weight."

"Not if I say it does not."

"What shall we do with him, then, if you do not want him and I will not take him?"

"You have never refused anyone before."

"But you have always been a dogmatic purest, never making even the smallest exception to your petty, little rules."

"You have always considered each soul you snatched a triumph."

I shouted, or tried to, but my voice was as before. "You made me what I am…was!"

"As always, you do not listen. No one 'made' you. You had the capacity of free will. You chose the life you led."

"I did not choose to have those enemies, having constantly to defend every scrap that was mine."

"No, they chose their lives as you chose yours."

"I did not choose my life. I was just dumped into it."

"As is everyone. You are judged by what you do with the life you have."

"You are omnipotent, you could have made it better."

The second voice broke in. "Omnipotent? No one is omnipotent. If God had had the power, Lucifer and the other so-called fallen angels would have been destroyed. Yet they survive, even flourish." "They" not "we?" Who, what are these...these voices? They speak as if they are detached from everything.

The first voice spoke, "No one takes any interest in you until you are dead. Everything you do before that is your responsibility. For what other purpose do you think humans would exist?"

The second voice, "We still need to decide."

The first voice, "I have decided. He is yours."

"I cannot, will not take him."

"You do not have that choice."

"I do. Do you want to stay here with him forever?"

"You know we cannot do that."

"Well, we have to do something to dispose of him."

Now I was angry, being talked about as if I were a piece of garbage and not a man. Again, I tried to shout but still the same uninflected voice. "Damn you! Damn both of you!"

And everything went dark and silent.

BECOMING SEBASTIAN

1

I opened my eyes. I was alive! Oh, thank you God! That was the first two seconds, then I realized that I was not in my room in Rome. I was lying on my back in a forest. The sun shone through the canopy. The soft rustle of the trees and the chirping of one or two birds were the only sounds. I sat up. Where was I? What was happening to me? I looked at my feet stretched out before me--except, they weren't my feet. They were dirty with ill-kept nails. I reached to touch them and the hands were in the same dirty state. Who was I? I scrambled to my feet. I was wearing rough peasant breeches and a loose shirt. They were filthy and reeked of sweat. I quickly became aware that the clothes weren't the only thing that reeked. Whoever "I" was, smelled as if he hadn't bathed in weeks.

Totally disoriented I could only ask again, where was I? Heaven? Hell? The Baptism of Fire? I thought the latter most likely. Before the doctrine of Purgatory became canonical in the 12th century, the idea of the Baptism of Fire, taken from John the Baptist as reported by Matthew, was held to be intermediate between Earth and Heaven, allowing souls not immediately condemned to Hell to be cleansed of sins. However, there was no fire and the trees and sun and birds all looked perfectly normal. Then I realized that I had no pain, indeed I felt great. Dimly, through the armor of my vanity, came an idea that I had sins to be punished, atoned through suffering.

I sat back down. I had to think. My learning in theology was not of a depth to permit me to answer. I wondered: Is God having a joke at my expense, dropping me down only God knew where or when or as whom? Was this body created just for me? Or was someone's body commandeered for my use? What did God expect me to do? Did God care?

Uh-oh, I was getting close to blasphemy.

After a time, making no progress in thinking, I realized that I had to get going. The shadows were lengthening. As I stood, I felt the shirt sticking to my back. Taking it off I found a hole between the shoulder blades surrounded by blood. Whoever had this body before me had been killed by an arrow. "I" was a dead man. God, presumably (if one can presume God's acts), having decided to return me--another presumption!—to Earth, used a recently murdered body. Very frugal. But it complicated matters. There were those who knew this man and someone who knew he was dead. If I walked into the nearest village, would I be recognized? Would the killer be there? I was certain that it was murder; if the previous occupant had been a criminal, the body would have been brought back to town.

While thinking, I had been looking at the body. Not bad. It was muscular; "he" seemed have had a life of hard work. It was huskier and, I sensed, taller than my previous body.

At that moment, I swore I was insane. At least insanity explained why nothing made sense. It occurred to me that Andrew's attack had not killed me. I was alive but delirious. It was equally insane that that realization made me feel better. It did not take long for me to be disabused of that notion. Everything was too solid and real.

I began walking toward the sun. I had no idea what was in that direction, but I had to go somewhere. If I were still in the area of Rome and if I were going west—too many ifs--it would lead me to the coast. Though I was barefoot there was no pain walking on the stones and branches. My "body" had belonged to one hard man. As I walked, I noticed that the sun was getting lower in the sky so it was afternoon and I was going west. For the first time in my life I appreciated my teachers.

Just before sunset I came across a stream. Finding a still bit of water, I looked at the new me. There was no resemblance to the old one. My hair was dark blond instead of black, the eyes were lighter, and the face was more long than round. The face in the water looked to have remained in the mid-20's. I undressed and waded in. It was surprisingly comfortable, wet but not cold. I washed as best I could, rinsed out my clothes, hung them on a branch and made myself a little niche in the bushes and waited for morning. I was not going to wander blindly at night. If my teachers had told me about the North Star and finding one's way at night, I had not been paying attention.

The night crept on. I was not in the least sleepy. Apparently, it is true that death is very restful. I had time to become aware that I knew nothing—who I was, where I was, when I was. I re- membered that my last day as Octavian was May 14, 964. How long had I been "dead" before I got here? I also realized that if I continued thinking about it I would indeed lose my mind. Eventually I went to sleep but woke when it was still dark. I groped for my clothes. They were damp but I got dressed any- way. Sitting in the woods naked was one thing I could change.

I wondered how I would eat and then realized that I was not hungry. As the sun rose, I resumed my walk. As the morning went on, I tried to keep the sun to my left, to what I hoped was the south. I was impressed at how panic improved my mem- ory. There was no path but not a lot of underbrush either so I rarely had to force my way through thickets. After some time, I wondered if there were any villages or other people. Was I even on Earth? Had I detached from humanity and my search possessed some transcendental, metaphysical meaning? I was not equipped to contemplate, much less resolve such questions. I kept walking.

After a few hours it occurred to me that I might no longer be human. I did not get tired or hungry, nature never called.

The sun passed its arc and began to descend and I hoped that I was still traveling in a fairly straight line. I am convinced that those who write of men confidently plunging ahead, guided only by sun and stars never had to.

2

Finally, about mid-afternoon, I reached a large clearing and to my relief saw men in the field. It was very bucolic, comforting, and above all, "real." In the distance was a sizable building with huts off to the side, behind a screen of hedges. There were several men, and a few women and children, working the field. The crop was just beginning to emerge so it was spring, whether the same remained to be discovered. I walked toward the buildings. As I neared, one of the field hands came to me and spoke. It sounded like German, based on my having heard the Emperor's troops when they were in Rome. I said "Italien" one of the few German words I thought I knew. He smiled, nodded and motioned me to follow. He led me to the large building which was the manor house and worked the heavy metal knocker. My guide said a few words to the man who came to the door and who then disappeared, closing the door. Since the field hand stayed, I did also. In a few minutes a well-dressed man appeared. I ventured a few words in Latin and was relieved to discover that though not fluent, his Latin was serviceable and we could converse. He asked my name and whence I came.

"Er...um...Sebastian. From Rome." I wanted to kick myself.

That was obviously the first question I would get if I ever encountered anyone, and among all my thinking I had given no thought at all to it. I hoped he did not notice the hesitation. In answer to his questions I said that I was a roving scholar, seeking to know the world and had been set upon by thieves who stole everything—money, horse, clothes. After talking among themselves in a language I did not understand, one of the thieves tossed me the garments I wore.

"I was luckier than the last man who wore these clothes." I said, turning to show the blood stained hole.

The more I spoke, the easier the lies came. My experience in diplomacy was proving very useful. More truthfully, I also mentioned that I was trained in both letters and arms and hoped I could find employment.

Arnauld, for that was my interlocutor's name, was a secretary and overseer to the lord of these lands, Lothair, whose seat was a larger castle about a day-and-a-half away. "In these uncertain times, trained men are always useful. The day after tomorrow, I am sending spring lambs and other provisions for the lord's table. You may accompany the men. I will write introducing you and if you meet his approval, I am certain he will have a place for you."

I was given a small room and was able to bathe and shave properly. Arnauld gave me a linen tunic that came down to just above my knees, undyed but clean; also a pair of sandals that almost fit.

I was taken to the dining hall where seventeen people sat along both sides of a long table. Arnauld introduced me to his wife, mother and three children—two boys and a girl—all looking under ten years old. He also gave a little speech which, he told me, recounted how I came to be among them. One of the others was the young priest of the manor village who apologized in very bad Latin for his very bad Latin. He had memorized the Mass but did not yet understand it all. "I know I am not prepared but the need for rural priests is so great that the bishop ordained me anyway. I am working hard to become a good servant of God." He passed between Latin and German, aided by Arnauld.

Among the others at table was the captain of the guard, his wife and his second-in-command. Also Hermann, a representative of Count Berthold of Breisgau, Arnauld's lord's lord, for such was the typical hierarchy of feudal fiefdoms. He was returning from an audience with Emperor Otto and would be traveling with us to Lord Lothair. I wondered if the emperor were the same Otto but did not ask; no point in revealing my total ignorance. I was seated next to Hermann, who spoke Latin quite well and had actually studied for the Church but decided on a secular life before taking orders.

Dinner was simple but plentiful. Mutton, turnip and cabbage —typical fare at the end of winter before new crops are ripe. Though I had not eaten in over twenty-four hours, I was not hungry but ate a good portion and declined more. I found the food and beer bland but was fulsome in my praise of both. My gratitude for food and shelter was genuine.

After dinner the children were sent to bed, the four women went off to wherever women go when they leave the men, and the neighbors left for home. The remaining five chatted for a while, haltingly since everything in German had to be translated for me and I had to be translated for the soldiers.

Shortly after I got to my room, an hour or two after dinner, the urge hit me. I had to get to the outhouse.

I have dwelt on this dinner because it provided the first indications of what I had become. Food and drink had no particular taste and quickly passed through my body. These thoughts did not occur to me that night but did begin to poke into the corners of my mind the following day when the same thing happened after breakfast and again after lunch. I was beginning to encounter, bit by bit, my future, but greater surprises lie ahead.

The next day I assisted Arnauld with the ledgers. He claimed little command of arithmetic but I found the books accurate. I entered and calculated the receipts and other numbers he gave me. I discovered that it was still May, 954. I had not been dead long. In fact, a letter from a bishop was dated "In the ninth year of the reign of Pope John XII." News of my death had not yet reached here. In the afternoon, I demonstrated my training with sword and buckler with one of the soldiers. It took a few minutes to adjust my new body to using the blade since this me was a little taller, stronger, and better formed than the previous me. My claims were being tested against performance.

At supper Hermann, whom I had not seen since breakfast, said that Father Henrik, with whom he had spent the day teaching Latin, would not join us. The Father had been called away to baptize a baby who was not expected to survive. After supper the family and soldiers departed leaving Arnauld and Hermann to interrogate me. I had been expecting this and had tried to be prepared.

Arnauld began, "You must come from the nobility to have had the training and education you have shown." At that time only the nobility had such opportunity and undoubtedly eased my acceptance. I was one of them.

"Yes, my family is minor nobility and, as a younger son I was trained to be an officer in the Papal army; my family anticipated that my broad education would enable me to rise in the Papal administration. After a few years as a soldier, however, I grew restless and decided to see the world."

"How long have you been traveling and by what route?" asked Hermann. That was trickier. I did not know where I was and had no idea how long it would take to get here from Rome. I did, at least, know that Germany was some weeks north of Rome.

"I left Rome about two months ago as part of an armed escort for a trading group to Milan. Since I did not have a great deal of money, this arrangement allowed me to travel and eat for free. And I was given a few coins when the goods were sold. In Milan I was approached by a nun who was taking a group to the Fraumünster convent near Zurich." I had had correspondence with the Abbess while Pope and knew it was in Swabia at the southernmost part of Germany. "I will say, the nuns were most impressive. The trek through St. Gotthard was steep and treacherous and the weather abysmal but they bore it like the soldiers of God they are and we made good time."

I was trying to give enough information to convince them I had actually done it without being specific enough for them to challenge me based on their knowledge. I was disappointed in my hope to distract them into talking about the nuns. Instead I was asked "And from there?"

"The nun who supervised the trip arranged quarters for the escort and I stayed two nights. I told the Abbess what I was doing and she was kind enough to give me a letter of introduction to the Bishop of Konstanz and general directions on the route. Despite her warning about traveling alone, I set out early on the second day."

"More courage than judgement." said Hermann.

"As it turned out." I said in what I hoped was a rueful voice, "but I was not expecting the thick forests and unmarked trails. The land in Italy is much more open and traversed by the old Roman roads."

"What roads the Romans built here," said Arnauld, "have all been overrun by the forests."

"It is only about 40 or 50 *milles* between Zurich and Konstanz," added Hermann "and I believe that part of the Roman road is still useable." He was well-informed, more so than I found comfortable. Was this accurate or was he testing me with false numbers to see if I corrected him? Having no way of judging I just plunged ahead with my story.

"I never learned. At the end of that first day, not knowing how close or far Konstanz was, I stopped by a stream to rest both myself and my horse, who had put in a full day's work. The next morning, just at dawn, as I was rinsing in the stream, I was attacked by four men." I did not recall having given a number in my first telling. "I was helpless, my sword lying a little way away."

"You didn't hear them approaching?'

"No. They were on foot and the running stream made just enough noise to cover their sound. I don't know how they knew I was there. Probably just my bad luck that our paths crossed. Although, I suppose I was fortunate that they didn't kill me. I walked for days—I lost track of how many—through the densest woods I have ever seen."

"You went through the Black Forest," Arnauld informed me, "I'm certain you agree that it is well-named." He gave a warm smiled, which relieved my concerns that they were trying to trap me.

"Completely!"

"You had a lot more luck in making it through. It is full of bears and the most vicious boars in Christendom." Hermann laughed and I felt I had made a good impression.

I laughed, too. "God watches over fools, which is why there are so many of us."

3

At dawn we set out for Lothair's. Getting ready that morning, I had been given another hint about this body. Though I had not shaved in about 36 hours, I had no stubble. I thought it odd but otherwise of no importance.

I had been given weapons and military dress as part of the armed escort. The party was larger than I expected: 8 soldiers led by the second-in-command, 7 men leading asses laden with provisions, Hermann, and I. I felt certain that we were escorting more than victuals because of the size of the group. There was something of significant value with us. I should explain that the cost of maintaining armed soldiers made 8 of them more expensive than the ostensible reason for our journey warranted, or else Hermann was very important.

We spent the night in a village, scattered among the house-holders. This was done so quickly that it must have been usual practice. We arrived at Lothair's without incident shortly before midday.

Lothair, who was almost 50 and one of the tallest men I had ever seen, welcomed us and turned the captain over to his chamberlain to put away the provisions, turned me over to his son, Josef, saying he would join me in several minutes and went off with Hermann who, I noticed, was carrying a thick leather pouch.

Josef, though not quite as tall as his father, was a strapping young man in his early 20's and he immediately asked me about Rome. I was duly impressed by how quickly Lothair had learned of me. Apparently a messenger had been dispatched from Arnaud the morning after my arrival.

Upon my complimenting him on his Latin, Josef said that he worked hard at his studies because he hoped to go on dip-lomatic missions as he wanted to see something of the world before he had to assume the duties of his father. With visions of imperial Rome in his head, he was disappointed that I con-firmed Lothair's poor opinion of the city. His father had accom-panied Otto to Rome when he was crowned Emperor, but Josef had to stay and manage the estates. He asked if I had been there and I allowed that I had seen the coronation. I retold my story and, upon his question, said I was a soldier. He was certain his father would have a place for me. I said I needed to learn German and he gave me a brief lesson until Lothair and Hermann returned.

Lothair was holding Arnauld's letter and said that I had had quite an introduction to Germany. I replied "I am not important enough for such a show and would have much preferred a more subdued welcome." We then talked of Rome and his time there two years ago. I was comfortable in reminiscing about the city I had lived in all my life when he switched topics suddenly to condemn the "lying, treacherous, lecherous bastard who calls himself Pope." Having heard all this before, I contented myself with mumbling that he was just a boy. Lothair was not placated. "He is a disgrace to his father, to the Church and to the Emperor! No wonder that he was driven out of the city." I nearly choked to keep from snapping that I had been brought back as soon as the Emperor's army left. One of the rare occasions when my brain was faster than my mouth.

Josef asked how old I was. I replied 23, not through vanity but as not to have him feel threatened by an older, more experienced man. Hermann looked at me quizzically and I added "A strenuous, outdoor life has aged me beyond my years."

He smiled. "That is true. It will. However, I was not thinking of your youth but how full your few years have been."

At Josef's suggestion, I was given the position of bursar making me responsible for feeding and paying the "army," as the six knights and eighteen foot soldiers were grandly called. He did not like numbers and was happy to give up the job. I also became the seventh knight, a special honor and an expensive one because it required horse and armor. I was struck by their ready acceptance of a stranger; then again, they had not had to cope with the treachery that was Rome.

Josef and I became very good friends, partly out of snobbery since we were among the few social equals. He soon told me he wanted to see Constantinople and the Holy Land and was enthusiastic when I offered to teach him Greek. Our lessons began with a Latin sentence which he repeated to me in German and then I gave him the Greek. We progressed nicely.

4

Lothair's overlord was a Count Berthold of Breisgau whose castle was on a hill in what is now the city of Breisach, Baden-Württemberg, overlooking the Rhine. He was engaged in a low-level war over a financial dispute with his western neighbor, Kolmar. Both cities had collected tolls on passing craft, but the year before, with Kolmar facing domestic difficulties from restive nobles, Berthold had seized a small piece of land on the west bank from the lands to Kolmar's south thus controlling both banks of the Rhine for perhaps 200 meters. Boats, which previously could choose either bank and pay a single toll now had no choice but to pay Berthold and cleaved to the east bank. Officially a purchase but in truth an extortion backed by threat of force. The Count of Kolmar, unhappy at the loss of significant income, was trying to drive Berthold off the west bank or take a bit of land on the opposite side. Both men appealed to the Emperor, but Otto ignored them. There was not time enough for him to get involved in every petty dispute among his liege vassals.

And now you know the origin of "Robber Baron."

A week after I arrived, fighting broke out again. Kolmar tried to grab a piece of the east bank just north of Breisgau, belonging to the Count of Falkenstein. Though it was not his land, Berthold was having none of it and ordered his fiefs to send knights and soldiers to expel the invaders. Lothair sent four knights, including me, and ten foot soldiers, under Josef's command, west to join Berthold. Simultaneously, Berthold sent envoys to Falkenstein, assuring him that he had no designs on the land and asking Falkenstein to join him. These "wars" were small affairs, often fewer than a hundred soldiers a side. The greatest European battle of the tenth century, Lechfeld, where Emperor Otto stopped the Hungarian invasion, counted no more than 10,000 on each side and no other war of the century engaged more than half that number.

With the contingents of Berthold and Falkenstein, we had 27 knights and 72 foot-soldiers. Berthold had given Josef command of the Breisgau forces, a signal show of confidence in a young man. Berthold's sons were too young to fight, but the fourteen-year-old came along as an observer. The Count of Falkenstein led his own contingent and though Josef had the larger force, he graciously allowed Falkenstein the nominal command and took the right wing. The Kolmar "army"—for want of a better term—was well dug in behind u-shaped breast works and showed no inclination to come out and fight. They did not need to fight; they won simply by holding their ground. Falkenstein, Josef and the commanders of our center and right conferred and decided on a full charge by the knights on a narrow section with the foot-soldiers running close behind. We charged, the knights in three rows of nine abreast, lances poised, directly into a new weapon, the crossbow which we learned later, had been introduced into France about thirty years earlier. The bolts which unlike a string bow, could pierce armor, took a terrible toll on the horses. Once down, a knight was an easy target as he struggled to get on his feet under the weight of his armor. About half the knights got over the breastworks. Fortunately for us, the Kolmars had not had time to put a ditch behind the earthen wall, which would have caused most of the remaining horses to stumble, ending in disaster. Their knights countercharged. I unseated two, but my lance broke on the second. I went to my battle-axe, which was my best weapon. The Kolmars had only about as many knights as we had remaining, and fewer soldiers. The drawback to the crossbow was the time to reload and the battle dissolved to individual fights with axe, pike or sword. We were pressing the foe toward the river when a shout went out among them. Looking up, I saw a barge approaching the shore, with reinforcements. Falkenstein, a large man who had been laying about to pronounced effect with a great broadsword, tried to pull us together to meet the barge. We were now not half of what we had been. The men of the barge, I would guess about twenty, began firing with their crossbows but were hampered by most of the remaining Kolmars on shore being between the barge and us as well as the bobbing of the barge on the river. The barge came to a halt. A bolt hit me below the collarbone near the left shoulder. Since it had not penetrated to the flesh, I left it in as a trophy. It soon was apparent that they were not going to disembark and fight on land and we were helpless to attack the barge so Falkenstein ordered us to gather what wounded we could and withdraw beyond the breastworks, back to his land. Josef had one of the foot soldiers retrieve a couple of the crossbows from the dead. The Kolmars did not pursue. As we left, I saw only two of their knights in the saddle and they were moving toward the river.

Back at Falkenstein's castle, a name more impressive than the building, we counted our losses: 8 knights, 23 foot soldiers dead and several wounded, as well as 13 horses, a very bloody result for a small battle. We estimated the Kolmars' casualties to be at least as great. The others were staring and pointing at me. I touched the bolt, smiled and said, "I'm lucky it wasn't any longer." Josef came up and pulled it out. It was longer. I could not understand how it did not penetrate.

Josef broke the silence, "The angle must have been perfect. You were very lucky."

5

It was now nearly dark and we stayed the night. Falkenstein had small rooms, like monks' cells, for his soldiers, and I went to the one assigned to me to get out of the armor and get ready for dinner. Removing the breastplate, I saw a large hole in my shirt, presumably made when Josef pulled out the bolt. I could not understand how I did not get wounded.

Understanding would come later.

Meanwhile, what to do about the shirt. I could not go to dinner with that hole. I went to the water room, a place which had a pump to bring water into the castle, then the latest comfort. As I left my room, I met one of Falkenstein's stewards, who looked at my half-naked body but said nothing.

"Can you find me another shirt? Mine is sweaty and smelly. I'd hate to wear it to the table." The request evinced a much greater fastidiousness than customary. The usual practice being to wear more perfume. The steward shrugged, went off and when I left the water room he was waiting at the door to my room.

"Thank you. You have saved me much embarrassment."

"It's mine. Please leave it in the morning."

"Certainly." And I gave him a coin from the few Lothair had given me as an advance on my salary.

"That is not necessary, sir."

"Of course it is. Just as if I rented a room or a horse." He accepted, bowed and departed.

The dining room was full, perhaps two-dozen, but subdued given the losses of the day. A priest led prayers for the souls of the dead and the recovery of the wounded.

Josef introduced me to Johanna, only child and heiress of the Count of Falkenstein, to whom he hoped to be betrothed. That may have explained his deference to Falkenstein on the battlefield. She was seventeen and Josef expected the marriage would be celebrated on her eighteenth birthday. She and Josef had known each other since childhood and had come genuinely to love each other, a love which survived the occasional quarrels between Berthold and the Count of Falkenstein. Berthold was not enthusiastic at the prospect of Josef, son of his vassal, Lothair, becoming an independent lord, even of a small and poor county. There were, however, worse options for Berthold and, while he had not yet given his approval, neither did he oppose the marriage.

I was seated next to Johanna's cousin, Mathilde, an orphan and ward of Falkenstein. My German was less than rudimentary, not having progressed much beyond "Where is my horse?" Nonetheless, we managed to pass the evening pleasantly. She and Johanna were about the same height, a little over five feet and both had blue eyes, Matilde's were lighter, leaning toward blue-gray. Johanna was blond and Matilde's hair a medium brown. Both were reasonably pretty, if not great beauties.

Mathilde was effervescent, moving constantly, and had fun with the sign language with which we tried to communicate. Even girls of the nobility were not considered worth educating beyond the domestic arts and social graces. Matilde, like Johanna, had memorized the Mass but was not taught to read either Latin or German. In any event, tutors for the girls would have been an extravagance beyond Falkenstein's slim resources. I found myself attracted to her and promised myself to apply myself diligently to learning German so I could see more of her and converse fluently.

The next morning, Berthold held a council of war with Falkenstein, Joseph and three senior knights—Josef included me, though I was not very senior. Berthold told Josef to send a message to his father telling him to reinforce the salient on the west bank, in case Kolmar decided to attack there to distract our activities here. Berthold also asked for more soldiers to renew the attack. Josef urged attacking as soon as possible, before Kolmar could strengthen its defenses. Falkenstein agreed. The small piece of land was important beyond its size because it was his only frontage on the Rhine, without which he would be forced to pay for access.

Four days were required to assemble a force sufficient to re-launch our attack. On the second day the Bishop of Kolmar, representing the count, crossed the river with a proposal for Berthold in which each side would evacuate the land seized and return to the *status quo ante*. Berthold refused. He felt confident of his strength and was very attached to the additional revenue.

Berthold somehow obtained a barge, added chest-high siding, which would, he thought, prevent a repeat of the reinforcements. During those four days, Falkenstein continued to have his archers harass the salient, attempting to prevent any strengthening of the defenses.

The first morning, after the council, Falkenstein introduced me to a peasant lad who was larger than Josef.

"Sebastian, this is Otto and he wants to be a soldier. Given his size, I think he could wield a battle-axe and you are the best man to train him." He then spoke to Otto in German. Turning to me, Falkenstein continued "I told him you don't speak German, but for him just to watch you."

He chuckled. "I also told him that while you knew what you were doing, you may not know what you were talking about." Otto had not cracked a smile. He probably felt that to laugh at the nobility was disrespectful, which would have been contrary to everything inculcated into him since birth. He bowed slightly.

He was a talented student. He started using the axe as if he were chopping firewood, swinging down two-handed. I had Josef give me the phrases I needed so I could explain that he had to swing with one arm because the other held his buckler and that swinging the axe across, as if he were felling a tree, gave more purchase for a stronger swing and a better chance of landing somewhere on the opponent. When we set off on the fourth day, Otto, outfitted from our casualties, was ready for battle and proud of his corselet, buckler, greaves, sword, and especially of his axe. He was at an age when anything looked better than another day working the fields.

6

I found ways to spend the evenings with Mathilde. I would sit next to her at supper and once, as we happened to enter together, she put her arm through mine and led me to the table. Quite the daring young lady, and I loved it. Without land or dowry, she was fated for the convent which, Josef told me, Mathilde did not want. He added that she would not make a good religious—she loved music, dancing and gay company. I wondered if he was hinting that my courting her would meet with his approval. I later learned that Johanna, who was close to her cousin, encouraged Josef to encourage me. Not that I needed encouragement. I counted myself lucky that I appeared to be the only eligible man close to Matilde's age.

On the third night, as I was lying in bed awake, which I did most of every night--I had found I needed only two or three hours of sleep a night. Not that I could measure it. Time was a much more abstract quality in the tenth century than it is today. Only the Church and some organs of government had any way of keeping time, often very inaccurately. The peasants and even the few tradespeople had neither method nor need of accurate time. There were no schedules, no eight o'clock Mass. When it was time, the church bells rang to summon the faithful. Secular life was much the same: bells and gongs called servants and soldiers to their stations, brought the household to meals. The basic timepiece was the sundial which would be "set" when installed at what was believed to be noon. An hourglass, then fairly new, was timed against the sundial. On an hour the glass would be set out with some fine sand in the open top. A servant would stand watch, adding a little more sand until the next hour was reached. The glass was capped and, voila, an approximately one hour timepiece. A passing cloud could force starting over. For nights and cloudy days there were candle clocks, which could be marked in quarter-hours, our basic unit of time. There were no minutes until mechanical clocks were developed several centuries later.

I was thinking about Matilde and realized that I did not lust after her physically as I always had with women. Was this true love? Sex had been one of the driving forces in my life but had not occurred to the new me until tonight and only as wondering why it had not occurred to me until tonight. I was discovering that my new body was very strange, it did not feel changes in warmth or cold, passions had banked. Strangest of all, I did not miss the passions. Perhaps the new I was purer than the original, but not, I trusted, to the extent of becoming a monk.

That evening at supper, I had swallowed soup without sensation while several others were complaining of how hot it was, reaching for cold drinks.

"Arrows that don't pierce, hot soup that doesn't scald. We have found a really tough man to be at our side." Josef observed to the table, with what I hoped was a note of pride.

Matilde came to my defense, "Yes, tough enough to conceal pain." That was followed by humor about our relationship, most of it gentle, some less so.

I turned my thoughts to the coming day and our attempt to capture the salient. That afternoon, Josef and I had spoken and I suggested an attack only by infantry armed with sword and either an axe or pike, using knights in reserve to prevent a counter-charge from the Kolmar knights. The crossbows took too great a toll on the horses, which were expensive to raise and train. I added that the infantry should use almost body-high shields instead of bucklers, affording more protection from the bolts.

Josef cocked his head and asked, "How old did you say you are?" Fortunately, he went on without waiting for an answer as I had forgotten what I had said my age was. Keeping track of all the lies was becoming difficult. "You talk as if you have commanded troops."

I tried to make light of it. "I wasn't always the idler you see before you. I was well trained from the age of sixteen. Because of my family's position, one of the captains gave me extra training in tactics and command. I also have combat experience," I laughed, "never ask me against whom." and was pleased to see Josef laugh.

"I can guess, but will keep the secret. By the way, tomorrow I will tell our men to try to pick up as many of the new bows and arrows as they can. I have been practicing with it and am impressed with how much penetrating power it has. I have had to use the same few bolts over and over so they are getting dull. I want a good number so I can find someone to make them for us." The first victim of intellectual property theft was whoever discovered how to make a fire without waiting for lightning to strike.

7

At dawn we set off, the first time I went into battle on foot. With only a leather corselet and greaves it was much easier to move than clanging about in full armor but I was sensitive to the protective deficiencies. As we drew close to the salient we were able to see Berthold's barge with about twenty men. Six were working oars and one a steering board. Bowmen were easy to pull together because all men learned to hunt at an early age. They were considered auxiliaries rather than soldiers. It did mean that more women would be working in the fields. The crossbow changed that. Training was necessary to become efficient.

As we got closer to the salient, we saw a barge moving from the west bank, but it did not venture into the current. Barges were designed to be poled, but the river was too deep so several of the men had to work oars. With only a makeshift steering board it was extremely difficult to maneuver. Both barges hugged the banks and were there to prevent a landing rather than engaging in the battle. But Berthold's was close enough for the bowmen on board to fire at the backs of the Kolmar defenders.

The defensive breastwork was a large semi-circle extending from the water. It was a jerry-built affair made of rocks, brush, and branches held together with mud. There was a large rowboat unloading supplies onto a small pier under cover of shields. Falkenstein's archers were behind their own makeshift barricade of brush and branches. Every day the Kolmar knights had charged, trying to drive Falkenstein's men away, but they would not cross the barricade for fear of their horses stumbling. Three days of desultory skirmishes had not changed very much. It looked as it did when last seen.

Berthold joined us this time, in overall command as well as commanding the cavalry, of whom there were only 14. Falkenstein had the center, Berthold's captain the right, and Josef the left. That was very elaborate for so few soldiers, but the noise and confusion of a battle required small units held together by a nearby commander who could be heard above the din. By my count, the Kolmars had only 11 knights, so a charge was unlikely, particularly as we had six pike men in front. The pike was a long—ten to twelve feet—thrusting spear, unwieldy and, because of its weight, very tiring; its great advantage was that with a sufficiently nimble soldier who could move to the side of a charging horse and by inserting the pike between its legs it was effective in tripping the horse. The numbers: We had, in addition to the six pikes, eight battle axes, 65 infantry armed with swords and 28 archers. The archers stayed in the rear a kept up a more or less continuous rain on the soldiers behind the redoubt. The Kolmars seemed to be somewhat fewer, but, once again, we would have to go to them.

We were able to gather only 23 long shields and we were the first rank, with two more behind us. We advanced as close in order to a phalanx as we could—our training and discipline were not up to Macedonian standards. As we lined up, Josef asked Falkenstein if the edge of the river was steep or shallow. He was thinking or running around the end of the fortifications. Unluckily, there was about a two-foot drop from land to water and a little more than that to the bed of the river. Geography was against us. We began our advance. Otto, next to me, was smiling and swinging his axe—the innocence and optimism (if that is not redundant) of youth.

The Kolmars unleashed a volley from their crossbows. I was surprised how powerful they were. One penetrated through my shield but when it hit my helmet the force had been spent and glanced off. While they were reloading, Berthold sent men with carpets to throw over the barricade. Otto was the first to scramble over with me right behind him. Their infantry opened to allow their cavalry to charge, but the pike men ran between the knights and thrust their pikes between the front legs tripping them. This was better than trying to stab the horse because the pike would not always penetrate the leather armor on the horse. After a few horses had been brought down, the cavalry retreated and the knights dismounted and joined the battle. I took my best swing at the first knight within reach and my axe cut through his breastplate and stuck there. The knight's falling wrenched the axe from my hand and as I was reaching for my sword a soldier drove his sword deep into my midsection, just below the sternum.

Which of us was more surprised? I have never answered that question. We both froze for a few seconds. His look of triumph as he pulled out his sword turned almost immediately to horror as he saw me standing and no blood on the sword. I had seen it go in but had felt nothing. He screamed. I thrust. He fell.

I had no time to think, the battle raged on. After an hour or more, our numbers told and the remaining Kolmars surrendered. I looked around and was relieved, indeed happy, to see that both Josef and Otto had come through. I did not have enough friends to lose any.

Berthold kept their horses, armor and crossbows, but let the survivors go without ransom. He had to live with Kolmar right across the river and tried to be as generous as possible. The horses did not fully replace those he had lost. Falkenstein reoccupied his land.

It did not take long for the men to notice the gash in my corselet. On the spur of the moment all I could think to say was, "Instead of thrusting, he tried to cut me in half and I was able to jump back just in time." I was depending on everyone else being too occupied with staying alive to have seen me. There was general muttering about my luck, several skeptical, wondering how such a cross-body slash could result in such a small tear. Not for the last time I was helped by the reluctance of people to believe what was clearly impossible.

The day was warm and the men were taking off their corselets to go back in shirtsleeves. I could not do that because the hole in my shirt would have been even more difficult to explain. In any event, my new body did not register heat and cold.

After tending to the wounded as best we could, Berthold and his men returned home. Josef and the rest of us, having a longer journey back to Lothair's lands, stayed the night with Falkenstein.

At dinner, talk quickly turned to my—choose an adjective: miraculous, incredible, impossible, unnatural, supernatural—escape. Matilde, bless her, ended it by announcing loudly "Who knows how God works?" Certainly, I did not.

Lying on my pallet pondering Matilde's question, I did not sleep. All the strange, even bizarre incidents since I woke on the forest floor—was it only 12 or 13 days?-- came together in my mind provoking even more questions. What had God done to me or for me and why? Was there a purpose to my existence, to use this gift to combat evil and defend righteousness, however they could be known? Reflecting on my life, I was under no illusion that I was the most appropriate vessel for God's work toward the redemption of the earth. As the night wore on, my thoughts wandered further. How many were there like me? Eventually my thoughts brought me to the Apocalypse. Perhaps God was preparing an army to fight the great, final battle with the Anti-Christ upon the Second Coming, widely believed to be on the millennium, now only a few years away. By dawn I had travelled to the end of my imagination no wiser than when I first lay down.

The next morning we set off to Lothair's, a sad procession of the weary, wounded, and dead; the last two groups laid out on a dray. We moved slowly, two horses, each with a rider, pulled the dray. Though the day was long at the end of May, it was close to dusk when we arrived home.

To our original contingent of four knights and ten infantry, Lothair had added two knights, six soldiers and fourteen archers for the second battle. We lost two knights dead and one wounded; seven soldiers dead, including two from wounds, and four wounded; no archers. We also gained a soldier. Otto, learning that I was a knight without a squire, asked if I would take him as a fighting squire. Because he belonged to Falkenstein— such was the lot of a serf—Berthold, who had been impressed with Otto's courage and ability, offered to send one of his own serfs in exchange. The deal was done. Now I had to find a way to feed, house, and equip my new squire as well as myself.

8

The next week or two were devoted to my various duties: Keeping Lothair's books, training replacement soldiers, working with Josef on our new languages, and assuming a large role in Lothair's correspondence since I my penmanship (quillmanship?) was faster and more legible than anyone else's. I got a knight's quarters which included a small room for Otto who was permitted to eat at the soldiers' mess. The knights who lived in the castle generally ate in the great hall. Most knights had a fief of varying size and lived in their own houses with family. My salary allowed me to meet all my expenses, as long as I was not overly extravagant. Because food and lodging were provided, the major expense at first was outfitting Otto and me with wardrobes. After that, save enough to purchase a fief, marry Mathilde and settle down. I was shocked, almost appalled, at how domesticated I had become. I was beginning to believe in the transformative power of love.

Then it began. In the fourth week of my new existence a pain, like hunger, but more intense and throughout my entire body. Several days later, the spasms began, my muscles felt as if they were being squeezed very hard. Mysteriously, nothing showed. In my room, I would look at my body, which was racked with the spasms, but nothing indicated what it was going through. Also, strangely, the pain did not affect my strength or energy. I had visions of mortality, thinking that this body was breaking down, or, since it was already dead, decaying. As days, then weeks passed, nothing changed. The pain was constant and affected my concentration, but I learned to conceal it, and tried to go about life as if it were not there. It was just part of my penance and the better I accepted and bore it, the sooner it would end—or so I prayed.

9

About twice a month, Josef would travel to Falkenstein to see Johanna. The first time after the battle I hinted, none too subtly, that I would not mind acting as his bodyguard for the trip. He laughed, "If I didn't bring you, Johanna would bar the door." I was grateful for the ally.

For Midsummer, Count Berthold hosted a feast and dance, a free-wheeling social event for the nobility, knights and their ladies, lasting from midafternoon until dawn, with the sole purpose of having a good time. I was able to renew my acquaintance with Hermann who was Berthold's *Kämmerer*, meaning he managed the household and treasury. Unlike other large gatherings, Midsummer was not tied to a holy day like Easter or Christmas, necessarily more subdued. The fourth great festival was harvest, which was spread out over the demesne and included all of Berthold's subjects.

The "orchestra" consisted of, as I recall, 2 lutes, a harp, 2 flutes and a tambourine and was of considerable talent. I remember the music as quite lovely but lack the talent to reproduce it and musical notation, if any, from that time does not survive. Dances ranged from stately to spritely and were group affairs, one switched partners often as the dancers moved around the room. "Close" dancing would have been most unseemly. I tried to keep an eye on Mathilde and managed to partner her more often than mere chance would have allowed. I was pleased to note that she was adept in placing herself in position for me.

During a pause in the dancing, Falkenstein took me aside. "I know it has been only a few weeks, but what are your intentions toward Matilde? Johanna is playing matchmaker."

"As soon as I feel that I can provide a comfortable life for her I intend to ask you for permission to court her." I am not joking— that was how such things were done.

"I thought as much. Look, Mathilde's happiness is very important to me and she would not have that in a convent. I'm not in a position to grant you a fief, but I think I can work something out with Berthold and Lothair. Give me a little time."

"Thank you. I shall be eternally grateful," totally oblivious to how literal that cliché would become.

The music was resuming and as we walked toward the floor, he put his hand on my shoulder saying, "You have my permission to court my niece." The next dance my feet did not touch the floor—or so it felt.

Had it not been for the pain, the next few months would have been among the most pleasant of my existence. Unlike Rome, I was not continuously being importuned for, oh you name it. Everything from blessing a child, money, a job, to granting a large fief, and, too often, needing to defend Rome and the Papal States from predators great and small.

One of those months, Hermann, Falkenstein, Lothair, and Josef spent at Aachen so that Lothair could report to the emperor and arrange for Josef's succession to his and Falkenstein's fiefs, which needed Otto's sanction. They carried a sealed letter from Berthold supporting such sanction and, as we shall discover anon, other arrangements.

Arnaud assumed the administration of Lothair's lands and came to the castle, allowing me to catch up on his family. He was training the older boy to become a scribe and accountant, like himself. The younger boy to the Church, the most common fate of younger sons of "good station" without the means to become a knight. Arnaud was also casting about for a suitable marriage for the girl and, unusual for the time, giving her a good academic education beyond the domestic arts that fell to girls. Father Henrik was becoming a very fine priest, tireless in his duties. Arnaud had had to curb the good Father's preaching on the imminent Second Coming, pointing out that the serfs' knowing the world was coming to an end in 35 years made discipline more difficult.

Faith in the Second Coming pervaded the last quarter of the

tenth century, from, as we have seen, the Dowager Empress Adelaide to the most wretched street beggar. Later, as the year 1000 approached, bands of pilgrims began walking to Jerusalem to be present for the coming of Jesus. When 1000 proved premature, the Second Coming was anticipated for the year 1300 with even *Doctor Mirabilis*, Roger Bacon, succumbing to the belief. But he, like Adelaide, died a little short of the big year, and thus spared disappointment. Undaunted by repeated failures, the recent millennial year found its group of believers in the Second Coming.

Three or four days after the Aachen group left, Arnaud got a message from Johanna saying that their *Kämmerer* had taken ill and could he spare me for a few days. Arnaud asked if I would mind going over. I am still amazed that I managed to say "Not at all" without emotion. I was torn between wanting to see Mathilde and the dread of the conversation I had to have with her. Otto was more demonstratively happy at the opportunity to see his parents and siblings.

After four months of intense study, my German was at about the level of a 7-year old. This was not a handicap in my job as all correspondence was in Latin. In the course of my four days there, I learned that Falkenstein was barely paying his way. The demesne was neither large nor fertile, being rock-strewn and having thin topsoil. He was able to cultivate grapes and the resulting wine, good, though not of the best quality, was his only source of cash or barter. He was, however, largely able to feed the inhabitants. He could just maintain himself as a knight with a handful of part-time soldiers.

The conversation with Matilde. When I was Octavian, sex was constantly in my mind and had to be pushed aside when I needed to concentrate on business. Over the months I had been here, I had thought of sex only when I made myself think of it. I had not had an erotic dream or an erection. I had concluded that I was a *golem*, a lump of mud, shaped like a man but not actually human. Bitterly, I perceived it part of my punishment for having been too promiscuous in my life.

Being alone with Matilde was difficult, there was always a chaperone, Lady Falkenstein or Johanna. By hinting that I intended to propose, they smiled and failed to follow us into the small room.

"Matilde, I love you, for the only time in my life I know what love is and it is better and greater than ever the poets wrote." She was smiling. "I want to spend the rest of my life with you, but," she stopped smiling, her eyes widened in alarm, her chin trembled, I was afraid that she would weep. Looking away, I went on, "but a wound a few years ago left me unable to have children," lies were now second nature, "I cannot fill my duty as a husband or give you the pleasure and satisfaction you deserve."

Matilde's eyes glistened but she held herself together. After a short pause and one or two swallows she said, "I don't care." I glanced up, her jaw was set and she looked resolute.

"But..." I started.

"Oh! No more buts. I love you for you, not for the carnal indecencies."

"But..."

"What did I say?!"

"Children. Surely, you want children."

"I have gotten along very well without them." Her natural good humor was returning.

"Then you will marry me?" I am certain there was a note of awe in my voice.

Very softly, "It is all that I want."

As we walked to the door, hand in hand, I warned that we would face the gauntlet. Johanna and Lady Falkenstein were waiting but neither Mathilde nor I said anything, just standing there feeling pleased. Finally Johanna blurted out, "Well? Stop teasing."

"She said yes."

Lady Falkenstein gave a little giggle, "You sound surprised."

I was.

10

In early November, the group returned from Aachen and I was summoned to Berthold's seat. The "other arrangements" of which we had mention, consisted of Falkenstein becoming a vassal of Berthold's, receiving in return protection, money to improve the land, and permission for Johanna and Josef to marry. Because Falkenstein did not abut Lothair's demesne, Berthold incorporated it into his lands and gave Lothair a smaller, but richer piece of land in return. Additionally, and the reason I was there, I was given that land as a fief and granted permission to marry Mathilde. Happy endings all around. I could almost forget the pain. Almost.

Berthold's stratagem was the beginning of a long process of aggrandizement by him and his descendants, eventually known as the House of Zähringen, accruing land, gradually rising to become the independent Grand Dukes of Baden, which was incorporated as one of the states of the German Empire in 1871. They ruled until the collapse of the empire in 1918, making them, at almost a thousand years, one of the longest reigning dynasties in European history.

Matilda and I were married in a small ceremony November 19, 964. Just six months had passed since I woke on the forest floor and I knew, despite the constant pain, that this was the life I was meant to have. And, despite the pain, I thanked God for this second chance, undeserved though it was. If pain were the price, so be it.

Because our fief did not have an empty house, Mathilde and I stayed in my apartment in Lothair's manor, where, in any event, my duties were. We spent the winter planning the house that we would begin to build in the spring. We did go around and introduce ourselves to our serfs, about thirty of them. The social contract was that they worked the land and the lord provided protection and food. The need for protection was more or less constant. Legally, we were all subjects of Emperor Otto, but he was far away and the various fiefs were largely independent and any weakness was seen as an opportunity for neighbors to encroach, so one would find an ally in a more powerful lord and attach oneself to him as a vassal with reciprocal duties and obligations. As a knight I was at the bottom of the landed hierarchy with barons, counts, dukes, and the ecclesiastic territories ruled by a bishop or archbishop, ranged above based upon their land holdings and pretensions. Actually, below me were the landless knights errant, basically mercenaries, trying to earn enough to keep themselves and, perhaps, a squire; when employment was scarce, they would turn to banditry. The serfs did not come into the hierarchy, they were just appendages of the land, and bound to it.

The pain was constant. Spasms racked every part of my body, yet I was able to remain more or less functional and rarely show it to the world. I would have done anything to be rid of the pain but I accepted that I was in some kind of punishment and would be released after my term. Such was the limit of hope.

11

In the early spring, reports of bandits began to come to the count's court. A small band of mercenaries, placed between eight and fifteen, without employment over the winter, had taken to living off the land. Count Berthold, in co-ordination with other local lords, sent out patrols to "show the flag" to the peasants and villagers and, it was hoped, intimidate the bandits into moving on. I was second in command of one patrol of four knights and twelve foot including my squire, Otto. This represented about a third of the knights and perhaps a sixth of the infantry that Lothair could raise and maintain.

We were always alert to other sounds. It was not possible for even a small troop of men to move quietly. The horses would clomp and snort, armor and weapons would jangle. As we proceeded, the birds would get louder and then, after we had passed, be replaced by others making a continuous counterpoint to our sounds. Anyone lying in ambush for us would have sufficient notice of our progress. Unless forced to fight, the bandits would run and hide. That suited us fine. Driving them away without casualties—ours, we did not care about theirs— was the goal.

The noise worked both ways. One warm summer afternoon the troop stopped to eat and rest in a semi-clearing near a small brook. In less than an hour, the men were almost dozing (in a few cases a little beyond "almost") and the horses were munching what grass there was. Then the sounds of horses and armor came. We roused ourselves quietly. The travelers were moving at a leisurely pace, a nice ride in the country. The noise came closer, evidently looking to water the horses. We knew they must be the bandits. Neighboring lords would not enter Berthold's domain without permission.

Lothair had joined us because he wanted to review progress on a brewery he was having built. He told the knights to take three men each and charge on as broad a front with as much noise as we could make, hoping to cause them to flee. The knights lowered their lances, the soldiers loaded their new crossbows, and we spread out moving toward the sounds, doing none of this quietly.

For some reason they chose to stand and fight. Maybe they

thought they could not get away without a fight. Of course, they did not know that we wanted them to run and would not have made any more than a token effort to chase them. Or, perhaps, we were between them and some objective. In the event, they charged us. Not a wise decision. There were, we computed afterward, thirteen and though they were all horsed, that was small advantage among the trees. Josef was like a child with a new toy and had trained our crossbowmen well. The first volley brought down six, and the knights unhorsed another two. An armored knight lying on the ground was nearly helpless until he could get to his feet—no easy task.

I had not unhorsed my target. We had both deftly used our bucklers to push aside the lance. As I was trying to turn my horse around through the bushes and trees, I was happy to see my opponent having the same difficulty and, in fact, his lance was tangled in branches. Our soldiers were reloading, which took over a minute even for an expert. My opponent released the lance and drew his sword. Instead of coming for me, he broke for the brook and escape. I was content to let him.

Riding past Otto, who was engaged with his own opponent, he brought his sword down and split Otto's helmet and skull. Enraged, I tore after him. Though the density of the trees made riding difficult, I slowly gained. Since learning that I was impervious to weapons I had worn only a leather corselet, just for show. This made the load on my horse considerably lighter. I had almost reached him when his horse stumbled in a gully and fell. I was so close that I was not able to swerve and my horse tripped over his. Although I went over my horse's head in a somersault, landing on my back I did not have the wind knocked out of me. There were definite advantages to this body. I rose quickly, drew my sword and threw myself at him. He had risen to his knees still held his sword and was gasping for breath. These broadswords were heavy and required both strength and agility to use properly. "Threw myself" was literal because as

I stood, my horse, trying to rise, bumped me and I fell on the bandit. My left hand grabbed his right arm trying to prevent his swinging the sword. A good tactic--he did the same. My right arm was across his chest so that my sword was only inches from his neck which I tried to slash. We were so close that I could feel his breath. He was strong and I was not getting any nearer his neck. He was pushing against my left arm and despite his disadvantageous position flat on his back I was having a hard time holding his sword away from me. While I could absorb stab wounds without effect, I had no desire to push my luck by seeing whether I could survive being decapitated. After struggling briefly—danger always seems longer than it actually is—I was able to pull my knee up a little which gave me enough purchase to push the sword against the side of his neck.

The blood spurted into my face and, gasping from shock, I swallowed some. The world changed. The rich, warm taste caused me to lose control and I bent down like some feral beast to suck as much as I could as fast as I could. In other circumstances I would say the results were miraculous, but let's say they were magical. With a kind of tingling sensation from my head down to my feet the pain drained from my body. Now on my knees, I luxuriated in the absence of pain. Physically and mentally I felt as if I were the most perfect creature ever. It was even better than I remembered sex. After some seconds of gloating, however, I was struck by what I had done in order to feel this way.

I heard myself scream "What have You made me!"

Lothair was riding toward me. I wondered if he had seen me drinking, but he said nothing. It was unlikely that he would let something like that pass. "You're covered in blood."

"I was right on top of him and the wound caused the blood to spurt more strongly than I could imagine. He and Otto were so young," I added hoping to explain my outburst, "I feel like a murderer."

"For better or worse, experience will numb your conscience and you will accept that God has made you a soldier and all which that entails."

No. God had made me something else, what or why I did not know and I questioned whether God knew.

I did not have time to ponder. I quickly checked my horse, which had risen. I walked him a little distance and was relieved to find he was not injured.

Then I walked back to Otto's body, knelt beside him, felt tears welling, but said nothing. I no longer believed in prayer.

The following nights were among the worst of my existence. I lay awake tormented by what I had become. I tried to console myself with the idea that it was a one-time thing, a kind of rite of passage, but I quickly dismissed it. I was convinced I was a dæmon, created to prey upon humanity and the more I thought about it the more fantastic and terrible my thoughts became. Was I a creature of God sent to punish a wicked world, or of Lucifer, gathering unprepared souls? If God was omnipotent, then the former, an omnipotent but evil God. If the latter then Lucifer was an equal power. Both explanations filled me with dread.

12

Character is a brittle thing. I accepted and stoically bore the pain as long as I thought there was nothing I could do about it. Once there was a remedy, my character failed the test. When, four or five weeks later, the hunger returned, my conscience waned as the hunger waxed and I immediately began planning to get blood. To my small credit, human blood was not the first I tried. On the pretext of getting meat for the table, I grabbed a lamb, brought it into a shed, where I could have the privacy I required, hung it by its back legs and cut its throat, letting the blood drain into a bowl. I drank and was immediately seized with pain and spasms beyond anything I had suffered, and vomited, seemingly more than I had ingested. No human could have survived that pain, but I did not even pass out, though I fell to my knees.

"Damn You! Damn You! Damn You!" For the second, though not last time in my existence I cursed God and Satan and all the angels, risen and fallen.

Standing, I vented my anger, frustration, and hatred by hacking violently on the lamb's carcass. When my frenzy ended, there were pieces of lamb strewn over the table and floor. A little calmer, I began to finish preparing the meat. I quickly learned that having to skin each piece was much more time-consuming than skinning the animal whole. And, though it did not occur to me at the time, I had lost a good piece of parchment.

I cleaned myself off as best I could, and brought the meat to the kitchen. With no one there I dropped the meat into the salt barrel—the standard method of preservation.

One more test of non-human blood had the same result as the first. I had no choice but to find if human blood would work again. Any thought of heroically bearing the pain was so evanescent as to have left no trace upon my memory.

Early the following Saturday morning, I picked up my new crossbow and told Mathilde I was going hunting and, depending upon my luck, might not be back until dark. By this time I had become sufficiently familiar with the region not to get lost. About mid-morning I came across a boy of 15 or 16 who was checking small traps for rabbits or squirrels. Later I reflected on his youth but at the time my thought was only of my pain. He was nervous and looked about to flee.

"Don't run. I'm just hunting deer."

Probably thinking I was another poacher, he relaxed and said,

"Haven't seen any, but I have two rabbits so far, with a few more traps to check." He held out his bag for me to see. I grabbed is throat with my left hand and with my right slashed his neck and put my mouth to the wound, almost a single move. I tell myself that he and most of the others never had time to know pain or fear. I drank and the result was the same. Everything was perfect. I now knew my destiny, but not why nor for how long.

I scouted around and found a small hollow where I dragged the body, put the largest fallen tree that I could move on him and spread leaves and pine needles until the body was concealed. If he were not found his absence would be put down as yet another young serf running away in hope of a better life. If he were found, what? News rarely travelled far from the immediate village.

I continued walking and perhaps an hour after noon brought down a roe doe, threw it around my shoulders and went home.

Lying awake that night, Mathilde asleep, head on my shoulder, I tried to sort out the experiences since I first woke up on that forest floor, now almost a year ago. I had my usual result—a stone wall of ignorance reinforced by total confusion.

13

Again, as at Rome, I was leading two lives. One was as a fairly prosperous and respected knight and landowner, happily married, and over the next few years, with increasing diplomatic responsibilities for Berthold, which I shared with Josef. In the fall of 971 Josef got his wish to see Constantinople. He and I, because we spoke Greek (Josef was assiduous in his lessons), and on the recommendation of Berthold, were selected by Emperor Otto to accompany Gero, Archbishop of Cologne, to negotiate the marriage of the emperor's son, Otto II, to the niece of the Roman Emperor, John I Tzimiskis. The journey was several weeks; overland to Genoa and then a boat to Constantinople. To us Franks (the name given to all western Europeans by the

Romans), Constantinople was an almost unreal fantasy. Home to more than 500,000 people it was many times larger than any other city in Europe. Hagia Sophia, even then more than 400 years old, was the largest and most beautiful building we had ever seen. On a bright day with the sun streaming through the windows, glistening off the mosaics, Archbishop Gero, as have so many others through the centuries, said that this must be how heaven looked. The imperial palace, though not so splendid, was sumptuous beyond our imaginations. We had never encountered anything close to such wealth and comfort. The negotiations were successful, despite some bickering over titles—the Romans maintained there was only one emperor and he resided in Constantinople. The fiction of co-emperors allowed us to conclude the treaty.

My other life was as predator. Necessity is the most effective of teachers. Once I realized what I had to do to be free of the pain, I settled comfortably into that existence and thought no more of my prey than does a tiger. By design or accident this is what I was and I had to make do as best I could, which, as it turned out over time, was quite good. But at the beginning hunting was a major inconvenience. Breisach was too small and sparsely populated for disappearances to go unnoticed. Two or three times a year a disappearance could be attributed to a serf running away, but I needed twelve to fifteen feedings a year. Unless close to desperation, I only hunted men. They were more likely to run away or be out alone. My hunting range was limited by how far I could travel. A good horse was capable of about fifty miles a day, half of which, if I wanted to get back the same day, did not bring me beyond Berthold's domains. I also needed time to conceal the body or, at a minimum, place it where wolves and other scavengers would mutilate it sufficiently that the slashed neck was not prominent. There were also days when I did not find a victim. My duties precluded my going out day after day, thus I had many days of pain. A long stretch would put a great strain on my self-control so as not to act precipitously with the danger of being seen. No one told me it would be easy; in fact, no one told me anything at all. My best cover was fighting. I tried to be on as many punitive patrols as possible but only occasionally would they coincide with the hunger.

The world went on without regard for me. The Emperor Otto died in the spring of 973, to be succeeded by his only surviving son, the 18-year old Otto II. Shortly before Otto I, my third successor as Pope had died resulting in rival claimants to the Throne of St. Peter.

14

We must now turn our attention back to Rome whence our adventures both began and next take us. Upon my murder, the Romans once again rejected the Emperor's choice, Leo VIII, and instead elected the pious, learned, and weak Benedict V who lasted one month. When Leo and the Imperial army appeared, Benedict submitted completely, allowed himself to be stripped of the Papacy, and begged forgiveness of Leo. In exchange for this craven display, Otto spared his life and had him carried off to Hamburg where he died the next year.

Leo passed his reign signing over as much of the Papal Patrimony to the Emperor as he had time for. Nine months later, before he had time to give everything away, Leo VIII performed his only service to the Church and Rome by dying. His successor to the Papacy was John Crescentius, John XIII, my second cousin (he was the grandson of Theodora the Younger, sister to my grandmother, Marozia) and the fourth Pope in a year.

John XIII managed to retain the Papacy for seven years, although faced with constant plots, revolts, imprisonment and escapes therefrom. On his death in September 972, the Emperor's allies in Rome elected Benedict VI, who was consecrated the following January. The delay due to the necessity of getting the Emperor's approval. When word that the Emperor had died reached Rome, the nationalist faction, led by the Crescenti, overthrew and imprisoned Benedict and installed an anti-Pope, Boniface VII. Otto II, tied up in a war in Bavaria to make good his accession, sent Sicco, Count of Spoleto. Satisfied with the work Josef and I did in Constantinople, the Emperor sent us, and a few soldiers to assist the Count.

There was nothing to it. After a reign of six weeks, Anti-Pope Boniface VII fled to Constantinople, having the unfortunate Benedict murdered on his way out and taking the Vatican treasury with him. Because the Roman Empire still ruled sections of southern Italy, there was suspicion that Constantinople had conspired with Boniface to extend its control. We did not inquire too closely, however, because Otto II was in no position to do anything about it. Sicco negotiated a compromise Pope, Benedict VII, my first cousin. He was the son of David, my father's younger brother. As I foretold you, in the tenth century the Papacy was the family business.

It was strange, even eerie walking around Rome, occasionally recognizing someone from my days as Octavian/John XII, including Benedict, but not able to say anything. In my mind and heart I remained Octavian regardless of the package. I did try to find Andrew, whether to kill him or thank him I never worked out. In any event I did not find him. Just as well.

There was the hunger and the sating of it. The state of communications—virtually non-existent—meant that authorities did not notice that five men vanished over the four months along my passage to and from Rome.

15

Time was claiming its portion. Hermann died in 975, Lothair in 980, and Berthold in 982. Arnaud replaced Hermann; Josef, now 43, succeeded his father; and Berthold's son, another Berthold, 32, succeeded his. I was the exception. Time, like God, had forgotten me. Over the years, light-hearted joshing about my extraordinary luck in escaping from seemingly inescapable situations had turned decidedly darker and now there was a bitter edge to comments on my "eternal youth."

In the fall of 983, Josef came into my office and closed the door. He pulled a chair close to me. He looked unhappy. "This is one of the worst moments of my life."

Now I was concerned, "What's the problem?"

Josef handed me the polished silver disc used as a mirror among our class, saying, "Take a look. What do you see?"

"I see me. What am I supposed to see?"

"Now look at me."

I realized what he meant. His hair was thinning, gray at the temples. There were lines around his eyes and mouth. He looked a man in his early forties.

"You look exactly the same as you did nearly twenty years ago when we met."

"You exaggerate. If I look young it is a family trait. My mother looked twenty-five into her fifties. Are you jealous?"

"I'm afraid this is not a joking matter, Sebastian. There are mutterings of witchery, of a pact with the devil. The soldiers are afraid of you. They say you come out of places where any other man would have been killed. I worry for your safety. It does not take much to bring superstition out of the ignorant peasants and soldiers and they now believe you are the agent of evil."

"Even conceding superstition, why is it attributed to evil, to Lucifer? Why not call it a sign of God's favor—though in my case that would be stretching it." I tried to keep calm, but the uneasiness about my age I had been holding back came to the surface.

"We are at a place where intelligence and good sense do not apply. You are my best friend and even I feel there is something unnatural about you. I do not want someone to run a sword through you to test if you are truly mortal."

Now I began to sense his fear. If someone did that and people saw no blood, no wound, they would go into a frenzy. Anything could happen.

"What can I do? I cannot wear armor day and night."

"I hate to say this, but you have to leave. No, hear me out." He put his hand up to stop my protest. "I have given this much thought and in a few days I will send you on a mission to the Emperor. Disappear on the way. The court has known you too long for you to go there without the same problem arising. I will take care of Matilde. I love the two of you as I love Johanna and my children."

I stared at him. What did he know, or guess? He spoke as if he already knew that I was something other than human. Or was I reading too much into his words because I knew the truth? Should I tell him everything, the whole story? Even if he believed me, what could he do? Lock me in the dungeon to protect the world from me? The hunger was a chasm between me and humanity. I said nothing. Would I have to leave Matilde, the only person I had ever truly loved?

"It has to be thus." There was a finality in his voice, his "Lord of the manor voice" giving an order. I went home to Matilde.

I walked slowly home, the house we built and in which I had been happier than I had ever thought possible. Even the killing, which I had accepted as my lot, had not shadowed that joy. Could I get through the next few days as if everything were the same as always? I was afraid that I would somehow give myself away or break down from the despair of leaving Mathilde. All the years of dissimulation and lying had not prepared me for this. They did serve, however, the next day when I suggested to Josef that we say that the court had requested my presence; that way, Matilde could not blame him or Berthold for my loss. He agreed. We set my departure for the day after tomorrow.

That evening, prepared with the story Josef and I had concocted, I told Mathilde.

"Why do they want you in Aachen?"

"I don't know. On the way I stop to see the Bishop of Strasbourg to pick up something for the Emperor. He may or may not tell me something."

"Sounds very mysterious."

"I may be just a messenger boy. Josef hears that someone from Constantinople is coming and I've had experience with them."

"What has the Bishop of Strasbourg got to do with it?"

"Who knows? Maybe something entirely separate."

"I think they should tell you what this is all about."

"I hate to disillusion you my love, but I'm not important enough to know."

Her eyebrows drew together, "I don't like it. Can you get out of it?"

"This is the Emperor. We want to stay in his good graces."

We left it there.

The day before I was to leave, as I was about to go home, Josef came and handed me a leather pouch of coins. His eyes glistened as he said "Please don't hate me. I wish I could think of some other way."

I embraced him, "I could never hate you. I know above all creatures the inexorable power of necessity." When we let go, I added, shaking the pouch, "I'll try to be more careful with these than when I first came."

He tried to force a smile, "Good luck and Godspeed."

Dawn came. It was time to leave. As I started across the courtyard to the horses, Matilde ran to me, eyes wet, and hugged me tightly.

"I am so frightened. Don't go. Just this once, don't go." I felt her trembling as she clung to me. We had been so close for so long. Had I given away some small thing she had picked up? Did she somehow sense, through that mystic, unseen bond between lovers, what I was doing?

"What harm can come to me? It's just a quick visit to Aachen. I have done this sort of thing a dozen times."

"Let me come to the boat with you."

"I'd love to, but then you would be coming back alone, probably after dark. It's too dangerous."

"I'm sure Berthold would let me stay the night." The determination and strength of character I loved was now a problem. Berthold had been told nothing. I was just going to arrive at the dock to get the bi-weekly boat downstream to Strasbourg. "Don't worry. Nothing can happen."

"No. This time there's a shadow. Oh, I can't explain, it's a dread, a fear I have never known."

I wanted so much to stay. If I did, only disaster lie ahead. Soon a mob would seize me and ...what? Condemned to the flames? Weighted down and thrown into the Rhine? Matilde was going to lose me. Better this way.

I kissed her, lingering longer than usual. My last words to her were, "I love you and will love you until the end of time."

A promise I have kept.

I rode away without looking back for fear, despite all the logic, I would turn and run to her. I was riding away from Matilde and home, God and Satan, now and forever alone.

ENTR'ACTE

B efore we proceed to those events of my subsequent existence that I wish to record, a few items need to be clarified.

You will have noticed, perhaps even commented upon that neither sunlight nor crucifixes have any effect upon me or that a couple of pages ago I saw myself in a mirror. Also, I do not assume forms like bats or wolves or become insubstantial enough to pass under doorsills. I cannot hypnotize or otherwise mentally coerce people, nor am I stronger than the human who had my body. Such aspects of vampires were, so far as I have learned, all the product of Bram Stoker's imagination. It was only in the early 20th century when I read *Dracula* that I learned of such powers. Dracula also aged or looked younger depending upon how long he went between feedings. I have only the hunger. I am grateful to Mr. Stoker because his depiction of vampires is so pervasive that I am able to go my way without suspicion as long as I do not linger too long in one place. Similarly, the term "vampire' did not widely appear until probably the 18th century, though there were earlier references in the folk tales of southeastern Europe. The first mention in English of which I am aware is John Polidori's *The Vampyr*, published in 1819, but his vampire, Lord Ruthven, does not have any magical powers, except immortality

As to my prey, I have found young better than old, the blood is richer, tastes better, and carries me longer between feedings. I can taste alcohol and other non-blood additives. I have become quite the connoisseur, blood is the only taste sensation I have and I make the most of it.

From the time I left Matilde I have used many names, most of which I do not remember. It will be easier for all of us, especially me, to keep Sebastian rather than to change names every few pages. Where a family name is necessary, one common to the nationality I am assuming will suffice.

In the course of these reminiscences, I will from time to time wander off to comment on events and personalities that for one reason or another have remained in my memory while much else has dissolved into a blur. I do not apologize these excursus. As far as I know, I am the only one remaining who has seen these things.

Much of my time has been as ordinary as yours, given up to the quotidian chores of existence, what Frances Cornford called "the long littleness of life." Only a comparatively small part has been spent stalking prey, disposing of the evidence, attempting to elude being caught. Until relatively recently I always needed money and every new personality I assumed had to find employment. While I do not need shelter, being insensitive to heat and cold, I much prefer the comfort of a regular home with a roof and bed rather than living outdoors in the rain and snow. I always needed transportation, horses in the past, automobiles now. I enjoy travel by car, train, ship, and plane; I am still in awe of being able to cover in hours distances that once took weeks or months. Some, though by no means all change is actually progress. I admit to being something of a fop and like to wear nice clothes. Also, within the limits imposed by my situation, I am a gregarious creature. I enjoy good company, parties, interesting conversation, theater, and concerts. In that regard I suppose I retain some human characteristics. Money is necessary to gain entrée into the circles I enjoy. While, on occasion, I have been readily accepted in those circles, such occasions have been the exception. Because my circumstances often required me to be an alien in the country in which I was living, most often I was met with indifference. For much of my existence I have been a low-ranking military officer; a clerk or minor official to a local aristocrat or landowner. Mostly boring and I moved on frequently.

Now let us proceed to some of the more memorable episodes of the rest of the story.

FINDING MY WAY

As the boat moved north away from Breisgau I was at a loss as to what to do next. I had never been this free, with nothing holding me or calling me. As Octavian my entire life had been governed by my birth. Waking up on the forest floor as Sebastian I had just wandered blindly until I was taken in by people I still considered my family and home. What to do? Where to go?

Late in the afternoon the boat docked at Strasburg where we would spend the night. The next day I took an early boat which landed at Mainz in the late afternoon. After securing lodging I took a walk around the city and met a priest whom I had known for a few years through my duties as Berthold's representative to the bishop.

"What does your wife feed you? You look exactly the same as when I first saw you...what?...ten, twelve years ago."

We chatted a few minutes before he pleaded duty and left. As I continued my walk, I realized that first, I had to leave Germany, too many people knew me; and second, that I could not again make myself prominent or as widely known. At this time I did not know how long my body would go on without changing. If this body were 25 when I acquired it, it would now be 44, definitely middle-age in the tenth century.

The next morning the boat resumed its journey and in the early afternoon we arrived in Koblenz where the Mosel flowed into the Rhine. In Koblenz I purchased a horse and trappings and set off to the southeast along the Mosel, which flowed northwest from France. Travelling upstream by boat was very slow and unreliable.

The next two centuries passed with little I have bothered to remember. Generally I was one of a large number of knights errant, going from one conflict to another—there was never a lack of demand for our services. France, the *Reconquista* in Spain, two journeys as a Crusader to the blood-soaked so-called Holy Land, Italy, back to Germany, the list seems endless. Occasionally a change, becoming a clerk or, rarely, a low level diplomat. As a knight, I had to move around often, my almost unbelievable luck tending to become even less believable with the passage of time.

Occasionally, in fact, I had to flee from a battle because of an escape from death that by no stretch could be called narrow, that even as accomplished a liar as I could explain away. Once, in a battle against a knight and wearing my usual leather corselet and helmet—I saw no reason to go clanking around in a hundred or so pounds of armor—the knight suddenly reined his horse. A longbow archer had shot me and the corselet was enough to prevent the arrow's going entirely through. The fletch was sticking out of my chest and I assumed the other end was protruding from my back. The archer was yelling but in the noise of battle no one could hear. I immediately rode away as fast as I could. The knight, either because he did not believe what he had seen or because he did believe and did not wish to know what I was, did not follow. Everyone else being otherwise engaged, I was not pursued. As I rode, I tried to pull the arrow out but after moving a few inches the flange of the arrowhead caught the corselet. After a few miles my horse needed a rest and I found a secluded glen. I scraped off the fletch and reached around to my back where the arrow was at a spot not easy to reach. After some contortions, which would have amused any onlookers, I was barely able to get my thumb and forefinger to pinch the arrowhead and a few more minutes before I finally worked it out.

I went back to wearing a metal cuirass.

A SEASON IN HELL

(With a nod to Arthur Rimbaud)

1

It was now the first decade of the thirteenth century and I was in London again making a living as a knight. Actually, I spent most of my time in northern France. The intermittent fighting between Philip II, King of France—he was the first to use that title, his predecessors styling themselves King of the Franks-- and John of England in his capacity as Philip's vassal in French lands held by the English crown, inherited trough William of Normandy, "the Conqueror," and John's mother, Eleanor of Aquitaine. It was all very confusing. I served under William, Earl of Salisbury, the illegitimate half-brother to John and who was called Longspear because of his great height.

In 1213, Salisbury had conducted a brilliant naval raid on the Flanders port of Damme where Philip was assembling a fleet to invade England. Memorable to me because I swung by rope from my ship on to the deck of a French one—very exciting and a lot of fun. One of my opponents made a skillful thrust and after the battle there was wide comment on my luck, of how so large a tear in my shirt could have been made without drawing blood. The raid ended the invasion threat.

The next year, John, the German Emperor Otto IV and various territorial dukes and counts seeking to break from Philip met

Philip and his loyal vassals at the Battle of Bouvines. Salisbury commanded the English forces, knights and archers at the far right, under the command of the Duke of Boulogne. King John was not present.

The French light (unarmored) cavalry launched a feint toward our left, commanded by the Duke of Flanders. The Flemings easily beat back the sortie but then broke and chased the apparently fleeing enemy only to face a counter-charge from the French knights. In the confusion, the left bent back, but the vicious, no mercy fighting lasted three hours until the Count of Flanders was unhorsed and captured at which the Flemish resolve collapsed. Unlike common soldiers, the Count's value in ransom or trade spared his life.

In the center, Philip and Otto faced each other with the major part of their forces. Once again, fighting was intense for nearly three hours until Otto, his horse having been killed, fled the field. Otto was alive to flee only through the sacrifice of many of his soldiers who fought to cover his escape until all were dead, wounded or captured.

As the French army wheeled to face us, Salisbury, reputedly the strongest man in England, was unhorsed by the Bishop of Beauvais who was using a mace in obedience to his clerical vow not to shed blood. Such are the quirks of fate. As I rode to help Salisbury, a French pike man crippled my horse, which fell. Before I could rise several soldiers grabbed me, removed my armor and marched me off with Salisbury as a prisoner.

I dwell upon Bouvines for two reasons. First, because it was the most important battle in which I ever participated, however insignificant my role. Before Philip II, the King of the Franks had a title and a small realm around Paris, the Ile de France. The English kings ruled the Angevin Empire which, in addition to England, encompassed nearly all of the western half of today's France. Bouvines made the King not only the most powerful man in France, but one of the most consequential in all of Europe. Philip was victorious in one of the seminal battles in European history and effectively created France. His was given the soubriquet "Augustus" in recognition that his role in the founding of the Kingdom of France paralleled that of the founder of the Roman Empire.

The losers continued to lose: Otto IV returned to Germany to be deposed; John to England to face angry barons and the Magna Carta.

Second, to which we now turn, Bouvines also led directly to the bitterest experience of my existence. Not being wealthy enough to be ransomed nor important enough to be traded, I was confined with four men to a small cell that we shared with rats and lice.

Morning and night we were given a bowl of gruel, which is every bit as repulsive as it sounds. Picture your morning bowl of oatmeal thinned with a gallon or more of water and used to feed five or six people. Of course, I had to drink the stuff so that my captors would not learn that I did not need food. Of course, it passed right through me. And again of course, the sanitation was practically nonexistent, a basin which was only irregularly emptied.

Time passed. The hunger came. Convinced I was a spy because I did not get sick or grow thin or get cold, nor did I show bites from the vermin, my cellmates drew away from me. They would take turns staying awake to discover when I would get extra food or talk with the guards. After four or five months—it was impossible to keep track—I was alone. One of others had died, two were ultimately ransomed by their families and one went mad, trying to chew his way through the wall. He was taken away, I do not know his fate.

2

A short time after, two guards opened the door. "Come with

us." I followed, not caring what awaited. It put a considerable strain on my will-power, just this side of the breaking point, not to attack and feed; the hunger was unrelenting. My will-power was bolstered by my not having a weapon. I was out of that cell for the first time since I had been thrown into it. We went up a flight of stairs and entered a room not much larger than my cell but it had a window. The cell had two slits near the ceiling that let in very little light and were too high to see out. Seated behind a table, a man in livery asked, "You are smiling. Why?"

"I am happy to see something other than the prison wall." It was now winter, the trees were bare but it was beautiful.

"Have you no family or friends in England? No one to ransom you?"

"No. I am a mercenary from Italy. The English are saving money by not paying me." I took my chance, "If your lord can use a well-trained knight, I am available."

"Mmmm. Interesting. You may have that opportunity." He frowned, "You seem to have borne your imprisonment well, most come out thin and weak." Having nothing to say, I said nothing.

He cleared his throat. "The celebration of the birth of Our Savior is two days away, and His Grace has bestowed Christ's mercy on you. You are free. His Grace did stipulate that you were to leave France immediately, but I will put your offer before him."

I was returned to my cell and an hour or two later the man in livery returned to say that His Grace could employ me but only for equipage, food and lodging. Otherwise, I was free to go without my armor or weapons. As acceptance was the only way I could recover those, I accepted. I also needed time to learn where I was and how to get back to Rouen, where I had left the money I had with what I hoped was an honest priest. But even this was complicated because I learned that Normandy, which had been John's, was now Philip's.

Also, I needed to feed. The pain and spasms were constant. If my travails showed on my face, no one mentioned it. That evening, after supper and being shown to my cot—in a room for four —I went hunting. I told the others that I just wanted to move after my long confinement, which was true. I was happy that they let me go alone, all having led a hard day. It was close to the shortest day of the year, so I could not wander too far afield. Very few were out on a cold night and I did not find anyone alone and out of range of others. I went to bed hungry, again.

The next day was Christmas Eve, duties were light, and we had the afternoon for reflection and prayer. I struck out for the woods behind the manor house, walking along a stream so as to be able to find my way back. Perhaps two hours later, about six or seven miles, I finally got lucky. A young man, looking not yet twenty, was standing behind a tree bouncing on his feet to keep warm. He appeared distressed to see me. Oh well, I was not looking to make a friend. I jiggled the knife from up my sleeve into my palm, walked quickly up to him and before he could speak, grabbed his throat with my left hand and cut the side of his neck, instantly putting my mouth over the gushing blood and pushing him to the ground. Ahhh, the relief, the exquisite feeling of pain draining from me, the only physical pleasure left to me. Then a shriek, a shrill scream. I twisted around and looked up at a girl younger than my victim, absolute terror on her face. The sight of my face, covered in blood, momentarily paralyzed her, but still she screamed, loud and piercing. As I rose, she turned and ran, shrieking all the while. I started after her and in a minute or two, when I was nearly able to catch her, we suddenly left the thick woods and were within sight of a small village.

Her screams had already brought the townspeople out and they were running toward us. I turned and ran, the crowd after me. I cursed the thickness of the brush which prevented any speed and drew no comfort from the knowledge that my pursuers had the same problem. Crawling between bushes, I came upon a pair of men, who grabbed me. We wrestled for a short time until the men from the village arrived, beat me with fists and sticks and quickly trussed me up. Pulling me to my feet, they pushed and pulled me back to the town, which was closer than I thought. In my running, I had somehow circled around.

"What's he done?"

"A cannibal. Elise found him eating Robert."

I squelched the pedant rising within me to say that I was drinking, not eating. I doubted it would help my case.

By now we were in the village where the fifteen or so inhabitants were making a commotion for twice as many.

The girl was being upbraided by an older woman, I assumed her mother, for being in the woods. The boy, Robert, was laid on a sideless cart with a woman, probably *his* mother, keening over him.

A man of about forty grabbed my throat, attempting to strangle me. "He killed my son and I'm going to kill him!"

The woman with the body yelled, "Kill him!" And then more softly, "Oh, my poor baby." She kept repeating these, punctuated by sobs.

The villagers were debating what to do with me. A pair of the more blood-thirsty were swing axes and yelling "Chop him up!" A morbid curiosity made me wonder what might happen. Would an axe pass through my arm or leg without severing it? And my neck?

Another said, "He's the devil. Burn him!" I struggled to keep a straight face contemplating their reaction as I walked out of the flames. You no doubt have noticed my arrogant assumption that naught could harm me. In retrospect, I had no basis for that arrogance, never having been chopped or burnt. In battles, when hit by swords or axes, none had struck in such a way as to sever anything. It did occur to me later, when I had much time to think, that perhaps I could be reduced to ashes. Then what?

That they intended to kill me, which I never doubted, was made plain when a group of four were told to dig a grave by the river, near the large oak. They were going to hang me.

I was pushed, pulled and beaten with sticks until we arrived at the site. The quartet was just finishing up the grave. The two in the hole climbed out—they did not want to miss the excitement.

The mob seized me, put a rope around my neck, untied me, threw the rope over a branch and some of the men hoisted me up. I put on a good show—wriggling, clawing at the rope, gasping and then going limp, what the mob wanted to see. It was now getting dark and I hoped the mob would leave me dangling there until morning and then, when all had left, I could cut the rope (I still had a small blade in my pocket) and escape.

The mob, however, had a different plan. I was cut down and thrown into the freshly dug grave. That was just as good. I stayed limp and allowed myself to be buried, thinking that I would wait a few hours and dig myself out. It was very difficult to remain still as the shovelfuls of dirt were thrown over me, particularly my face. Eventually it was finished and I waited until I thought that it was late enough for my resurrection.

3

I was able to bend my knees a little to create a small space under my hip, smaller than I intended--the dirt was very heavy —but I managed to keep some space, which served no purpose whatsoever. A while later, when I was certain the crowd had gone, I began scratching with my fingers hoping somehow to dig myself out and discovered that, despite all the stories, you cannot. You need someplace to put the dirt you are trying to dig and get it out of the way in order to move. Extra space was what I definitely did not have.

And time seeped away.

Buried alive for years, centuries, I could not remember. I had lost all sense of time. It seemed forever. All I had were memories of light and air and freedom. And the hunger. Always the hunger, the pain, the spasms, the lust for blood, so intense they must kill me. But I lived on, and on, and on. For a while I hoped this was my term of punishment, Baptism of Fire, Purgatory, or whatever God decreed. Eventually I reconciled myself to the knowledge that there would be no end and that this was Hell. Was this the way it was supposed to be? Should I have borne the hunger even after learning about blood? Perhaps that was my penance and I had failed. I was a murderer. It was so unfair! I had simply been tossed in this situation without a word. How was I to know the rules?

There was nothing but silence--no voices this time, no chance to argue my cause.

Time passed, filled with pain and anger, resignation and self-pity, praying to escape, praying to die. I passed time by trying to remember everything I had ever known in all the languages I knew.

And then it was over. The dirt turned to mud as it had often done. That rain falling was comforting, reassuring me that I was still part of the larger earth, beyond this damned hole. Less comforting was the feeling that I was a plant being watered.

What was that? I thought I felt a movement at my left shoulder. I tried to move and was surprised to discover that I could, a little. I wiggled a while and became conscious of another sensation on my shoulder. It was wet. I scarcely remembered the feel of water, water that was now washing away my prison.

Gradually, excruciatingly slowly the dirt was loosened. My left arm was free and I furiously clawed away the dirt on top of me. Almost free, I was suddenly torn from the grave and swept along by the flooding river. There was no light save frequent lightening, no sound except the roaring river and peals of thunder.

Though helplessly pulled along by the water, I was buoyed and happy at the light and sound. I had greatly missed them and was happy beyond anything I had known to be free.

Abruptly I bumped into land. Feeling myself being pulled away, I reached out blindly in the dark and found a branch and grabbed hold. With strength found in desperation, I dragged myself to higher ground. I was even more grateful for this body, having been immobile for what seemed forever, it was as flexible as the day I was buried.

Time passed. The storm did not lessen. I enjoyed the rain, wet was one of the few physical sensations left to me and the first since the mob had buried me. The occasional lightening flash would have revealed me face up and smiling. The river was close, heard more than seen.

After a time, dawn came. Because of the rain and clouds, it was a dark dawn but I was now able to make out the silhouettes of trees and houses. I heard, or thought I heard a shout from the river. I moved to the edge of the water, holding the branch of a tree to avoid slipping on the mud and back into the river. I saw the figure, a person lying prone on a large piece of wood. I yelled and waved. The man saw and in trying to wave, slid off the wood. Luckily, the current was bringing him closer to me and, clinging to the branch, I stepped carefully into the water. Now sure of my footing, I extended my body stretching out an arm and as the man was going by, we managed to grasp wrists. I was almost pulled in, but the branch held and I was able to pull the man to the bank.

The man gasped for air and said, "Thank you, sir. Thank you."

A few more gasps. "I was sure I was gone. I owe you my life."

I collected.

4

It was now light enough to orient myself. The first thing I noticed was that my clothes had not borne the interment as well as my body had. They were torn and moldy. I took those of my victim, and though he was a little smaller than I they would serve until I could do better.

Where was I? When was I? I remembered that I was in France, Flanders—or had been when I was buried. To whom did it belong now? How long had I been buried? I was back at the beginning, laying in the woods, asking myself questions I could not answer. I began walking, going with the flow of the river knowing it would take me someplace and that there I would cope, as I always had.

As I walked, reflecting upon my ordeal, I realized that I was angrier than I had ever imagined I could be. I resolved never to be captured again. I would kill until I went down or my tormentors fled in terror on discovering they could not kill me.

After about an hour, I came across two men, one older, one younger trying to pole a scow from the bank against the current of the river. I offered to help in exchange for a ride.

"Where are you going?" the older man and I said this almost simultaneously. Since I had no answer, I was happy that he supplied one.

"Tournai."

I beamed, or hoped I beamed, "My destination. Can you use another hand?"

"Gladly. I have lived along the Scheldt my entire life and never seen it this high."

I boarded and grabbed a pole and with an effort we managed to shove off.

"Why are you making such a dangerous trip?"

"Money. I have a load of raw wool and I figure if I get to market before anyone else, I will be able to sell it all for a good price. I have only about 60 sheep and I have to beat the large landowners."

Shearing season. It was spring. As we went along the rain lessened and I learned the men were father and son. From my still fertile imagination: I was an Italian traveler who had been on a boat going to Tournai when it had struck a tree that had fallen into the river. We capsized and I, being a strong swimmer, made it to shore but the boat with my belongings had disappeared and I did not know the fate of the crew and other passengers.

"A very foolish man to take his boat out on this river." He smiled to show he recognized the irony.

"When we boarded, yesterday morning, none of us thought it would get this bad and we were all impatient to get to Tournai." He frowned but said nothing. I told myself not to talk too much —I had no idea what yesterday morning was like.

We were making good progress as the river was swift. And in two or three hours we were at Tournai. With some effort and help from men at the pier, we put in. They offered to share lunch with me, but I said that I had friends here and did not need to call further on their hospitality. With mutual wishes of good luck, we parted and I walked away from the river toward the cathedral, whose spire was visible.

While I did not know how long I had been buried, I was certain that it was a very long time. You may be wondering what changes I noticed as I walked through the streets. None. Accustomed to the constant change of the last two centuries, people today probably cannot appreciate how slowly the world moved between the tenth and eighteenth centuries. The lives of the common people still lived to the rhythm of the seasons. Farm chores and cottage crafts remained virtually unchanged year after year, century after century. Only the fashions of the nobility changed, but that affected only the top one percent who, like the poor, are always with us. In the eight centuries between my birth and the invention of the steam engine, the only truly history changing invention was the printing press.

Now that I knew where I was, there remained to discover when. I shrank from walking up to someone and asking— I would be marked a lunatic or, at the least, attract attention and cause comment, which I wished always to avoid. Calendars did not hang on every wall, life then being more attuned to the ecclesiastical year. One was in Lent or Pentecost or Advent or another of the markings of the Church. Only the Church or the Court needed to know the date or even the year.

5

By this time I had reached the cathedral, Notre-Dame, which has somehow survived wars and revolutions for 900 years and looks today very much as it did when I first saw it. When I knocked, the Rectory door was opened by an elderly (maybe 60) nun who looked at my poor and ill-fitting clothes and told me that I could go to the back for something to eat.

"Thank you, Sister, but I am not here for food. I am a wandering scholar and have lost all my possessions to the river. I hope that Monseigneur will find me worthy of a recommendation for a position."

"Where are you from?" She got the same story I had given the boatmen.

"Ahhh, I thought I detected a bit of an accent. The Bishop is away but will be back for Sunday Mass. I will ask his secretary to see you."

"You are most kind. Since I am just arrived, may I ask the name of your bishop?"

"Jean de Vassogne. He has been here almost five years. Please come in while I find Monsieur Gilles." So, Gilles was a layman.

She motioned to a chair in the foyer and I took a seat while she went through a side door. A few minutes later, through the same door, a man of 30 to 35, entered.

"Good morning, sir. I am Gilles de Vassogne, secretary to my uncle, Bishop Jean de Vassogne." Nepotism was still in fashion.

"Good morning, my name is Sebastian and I am grateful you have consented to see me."

He knitted his forehead, "Is Sebastian your given name or family name?" That was a change. While I was "away" names had become more detailed, instead of being Sebastian son of Robert, family names had come into use. Before I had been Sebastian from where ever I was from at that time so I chose a place near Rome.

"I beg your pardon. Sebastian di Tivoli." I told my story yet again, adding that I possessed an excellent education and was literate in Latin, Greek, Italian, French, and German, also proficient in arms and that I was looking for employment.

"Soldiers are always needed. The king is in Gascony fighting against the English." Still? Again? I did not know what it was that I was supposed to know and dared not ask for details. He did not volunteer any.

He continued, "If you do not mind, I have a favor to request based on your knowledge of Greek. Several days ago an elderly and sick monk from the war zone stopped here for help but it was too late and he went to Jesus the next morning. Among his few possessions was a parchment in what looks like Greek. Could you look at it and translate?"

"Certainly, I would be pleased to help."

"Follow me." We went through the door he had entered into a hallway. After a short distance we entered what looked to be an office. Gilles went to a drawer of a cabinet, carefully took out a sheet of parchment, less than a foot wide and perhaps 8 inches long, and smoothed it out on the table. After inspecting it for a few minutes, I began to translate.

"Down the rocky face of the mountain
    Came Poseidon with great, speedy steps
    And the rising hills and tall trees shook...

It is from The Iliad, but only twenty lines. I wonder where the rest of it is."

"That is probably all the abbey had. I should think the monk would rescue all that there was. Would you be kind enough to write a translation? It will please the bishop when he returns." He went to another drawer and brought a sheet of paper and pointed to the stylus and ink well on the table. Paper had just begun to be widely used when I was at Bouvines; now, seemingly, it was common. "I have some correspondence to write." He sat on the other side of the table a little beyond my right. For a while there was no sound except the scratching of our styli. It was very comforting, giving me the sense that I was indeed back in the world.

When I had finished, Gilles took the translation and gave me a look somewhere between astonishment and disbelief. "Where did you learn to write like this?"

Having no idea what he meant, I said from an old tutor when I was a child.

"I have not seen writing like this on documents much less than a hundred years old." He handed me one of the sheets he had written. It was quite different, but I could read it.

All I could think of to say was "I learned to write in a small, isolated monastery. New trends were slow to get there."

I later learned that during my absence, the Carolingian uncial script I had learned had been largely replaced by Gothic, also called black letter. As I often have, I thought "Why can't they just leave well enough alone?"

Gilles, who had taken a liking to me, had the elderly nun, Sister Helene, prepare me a room. He apologized that it was in the servant's wing and I assured him it was much better than my recent quarters.

The next day, Gilles allowed me paper, ink and a part of the desk to practice the new script. I changed my mind about change. From one of the documents that Gilles gave me to transcribe, learned that it was 1396, the seventh year of the pontificate of Boniface IX.

My temples throbbed with anger as I experienced a visceral reaction, a reversion to my suffering. One hundred and eighty-two years! Lying in that hole for 182 years! The hunger had never abated. The pain, the spasms never lessened. I now understood that there was to be no end to the hunger. God and Satan, one or both, had put me upon the earth to be a scourge, a blood-thirsty predator. Why, I could not even begin to fathom. Had my sins been so great? I thought not, but then I was probably not the best judge. How long? I recalled the words of Isaiah, "Until cities lie in ruins without inhabitants, houses without men, and the land is ruined and desolate." Was I an instrument to bring that day?

Gilles brought me back to the present. "Are you all right. You do not look well."

I paused a few seconds, both to calm down and to choose among an assortment of lies. "It will pass. When I was in the river something crashed into me." I rubbed my side, "My ribs are sore and occasionally will give an extra-sharp pain. Normally, it hurts only when I breathe." I forced a smile to show that this was humor. "Nothing is broken so it should mend in a day or two." We went back to our tasks.

Bishop de Vassogne returned about noon Saturday. Gilles explained my presence. His Excellency observed that God was watching over me. I suppressed an urge to contradict him. He did not seem displeased that I was there and thanked me for the translation, regretting that he had not learned Greek. Over lunch he questioned me. He then said he had been to Rome a few years earlier and asked if I had seen the city. The truthful answer would have been "Not for more than 200 years," so I said no, that I was from Savoy and had never been to Rome. At mid-afternoon he said that the Count of Auteuil was looking for someone to take care of his administrative duties and he would give me a letter of introduction, though not a recommendation since he did not know me well enough to give an honest one. I thanked him. He kindly asked Gilles to take me to the local tailor to make me presentable for the interview. I thanked him again.

The Count was not yet 30 and had inherited title and lands the previous year. We hit it off—he thought we were about the same age. One of my qualifications was that I had combat experience. I said I was rusty as I had not been able to train for a few years but was certain I could get back my proficiency quickly. I began almost immediately but did not stay long. Hunting was much easier in the cities than in a rural area like Auteuil. Less than a year later I went to Paris, scrapped by with odd jobs, attended classes at the university, and fed well in a city of close to 300,000 people, many rootless and new to the city.

PADERBORN

The Thirty Years' War

I came to the Bishopric of Paderborn, in the German Rhineland, in the late 1630's after having served a little over a year in one of the Catholic armies. I had secured an appointment as a junior seneschal under the Prince-Bishop, Ferdinand, a younger son of the Duke of Bavaria. Paderborn was one of the five sees that Ferdinand held. His real power derived from being Archbishop-Elector of Cologne; thus, he rarely came to Paderborn which he entrusted to his governor, Bishop Dietrich von der Recke, with whose brother I had served and who had recommended me.

Paderborn had been sacked in 1622 and the treasury plundered by a Protestant army. The condition of the city only deteriorated further in the ensuing twenty years of war. This was the situation when I arrived. My position was the equivalent of being a police precinct captain, charged with maintaining order in a section of the city. Other duties included collecting taxes and defending the city in case of attack. The latter, fortunately, did not occur; the former did not give me many friends as the exactions were necessarily steep to keep Ferdinand's army in the field. The only fighting was against an occasional party of foraging soldiers in the country side. As usual, my luck in surviving dangers roused comments.

I got on very well with the Bishop, moving beyond my official duties to help in the Chancery because of being literate in several languages. Elector-Archbishop Ferdinand asked twice for me to move to Cologne and head his Chancery. Because I always avoid prominence—never wanting to be important enough to be searched for when I inevitably disappeared--I begged off, saying I was not suited to sit at a desk writing all day and hinting that I was pursuing a romance in Paderborn. In 1646 I was promoted to Seneschal, which is Chief of Police.

The weight of poverty, taxes, hopelessness, and the terror of another attack made Paderborn a sad and angry place, no different from most in Germany. About a year before the war finally ended that anger was directed, as so often happens, against the Jews. After several days of individual acts of vandalism, one evening towards dusk, the daughter of Benjamin the cobbler came pounding on my door screaming "They're hurting papa, they're hurting papa!"

Like most of the children in town, poor nutrition made her small for her age of about 12.

I grabbed my sword and buckled it on as I ran after her to the shop. A crowd of 20 to 25 was yelling encouragement to three men who were pummeling the cobbler. I stood between them and shouted "Stand back!" three or four times. I saw one of the parish priests.

"Father, help me calm the crowd. He is a poor worker just like them. Why attack an innocent man."

"No Jew is innocent. They are all guilty in the blood of Jesus."

I shouted angrily, "Father, do you not understand the first thing about Christianity?"

"I may not be so well educated as our seneschal," he spoke more to the crowd than to me, "but I know the Gospel and the

Crucifixion."

"I did not ask if you know, but if you understand." I raised my voice to be heard, at least by those in front. "The first thing about Christianity is the Resurrection. St. Paul said '...if Christ has not been raised, then our proclamation has been in vain and your faith has been in vain.' Also, the passages in the Old Testament foretelling Jesus nearly always speak of His suffering and dying. God's plan for the redemption of Man required the Passion and Crucifixion of Jesus who is, after all, a manifestation of God and could easily have saved Himself. His passion and death were His way to show his eternal love for Man and point the way to ultimate salvation. Those whom God chose to carry out his work are guilty of nothing but obedience to the plan of God."

Someone shouted "He thinks he's the Pope!" The crowd had quieted, but a few laughed softly. I smiled. Father Lorenz looked surprised, whether because he had never thought of it or at the fact that I knew it, I never discovered.

One of the others spoke. "People have disappeared over the last few years. Sacrificed by the Jews, no doubt. What other explanation could there be?"

An awkward question. I was not going to give them the "other explanation." While I generally preyed over a wide area to avoid talk of disappearances, sometimes it was necessary to grab a local. However, long practice had given me a ready-to-use explanations.

"The men left to look for work rather than starve here." I had been careful to choose the idle. "And the Shirtz girl ran after that soldier she was in love with. We conducted a thorough investigation and the authorities are satisfied."

Three deputies had joined me and whatever their feelings towards Jews, they were not going to risk the few groschen they earned. While I had been speaking to the crowd, Bishop von der

Recke had arrived and having spoken with Father Lorenz, came to my side and spoke to the crowd.

"Our Jewish neighbors have done no harm of which I am aware. Those who can, like the rest of you, work hard and pay their taxes. Please go home and reflect upon your conduct that it will not be repeated." It was now dark and the crowd broke up quickly. We left together.

Von der Recke was a plump man with a round face adorned by an elaborate mustache curled at the ends and a narrow, though thick goatee from under his lower lip to the bottom of his chin. As we walked, I thanked and complimented him for his tolerance. He chuckled. "His Highness would not look kindly upon the loss to his purse. Several of our Jews have little shops, enabling them to pay both the regular taxes plus the Jewish entail." He did not need to add that his income would also be affected, from which, to be honest, my salary was paid.

"Perhaps," I said, "word should be passed that if the Jews are driven out everyone's taxes would go up to cover the shortfall."

He stopped, turned towards me and nodded slowly two or three times. "You are subtle and devious enough to have had a fine career in the Church. What you said to Father Lorenz is theologically correct and indicates a good education. The Trinity is not an easy concept. Did you once study for the Church?" Our previous conversations had been mostly about my duties.

"As a child of some privilege, I had the advantage of an excellent education: Latin, reading, writing and rhetoric. And training in arms. It is the last which has afforded me regular employment. The war has destroyed much and changed everything. I cannot go back to the home of my youth." Experience has enabled me to speak truth without being truthful.

"Aaahh. I have noticed that you spend time in the palace library. You are still young. I encourage you to open yourself to the Holy Spirit that you may receive the calling."

"In these terrible times, Father, my skills are perhaps better employed in physical rather than intellectual battle with the heretics."

"That is the unfortunate truth. I regret that reason has not prevailed and that violence becomes necessary."

We walked slowly, "You know," he continued, "those people have much more in common than they know. They all struggle to keep food and shelter for themselves and their families. It is a failure that we do not teach them."

"No, My Lord, not a failure. It is in the interest of those who rule that the poor should hate each other rather than hate them."

He stopped again. "You are very cynical for a young man."

"I have seen much in my years to make any man cynical." If he knew how much! And how many years!

"Yes, the war has affected many that way. Do not let it shake your faith that God is just and that the scales will be balanced eventually; perhaps not in this world, but eventually."

Small comfort to those being ground in misery. Faith gives one the serenity to believe that everything will come right in the end. These thoughts, of course, remained unspoken. I did say, "Not if Father Lorenz and his kind have their way. I cannot understand his lack of even a little compassion, surely a min-imal requirement for one claiming to be a servant of God."

The Bishop gave a small shrug, "God made him a fool. Who are we to question the work of God?"

The next year, peace was finally signed. After thirty years of war each side was left much as they started in land. However, the losses in life, treasure and the damage to the psyche of the people scarred Germany for centuries.

I left Paderborn the year after, having begun to hear "He never changes."--always the impetus to travel on.

A few years after I arrived in Paderborn, von der Recke had asked me to take a boy of 16, Konrad, and tutor him in arms. Konrad's father had been a friend of the Bishop and had fallen in Ferdinand's service a few years before. The boy was an indifferent student in the church school and did not have the vocation to go into the priesthood. The Bishop felt that being a soldier was his best opportunity. Konrad was most certainly not an indifferent student for me. He took to the training quickly and happily, willing to do whatever work that would make him better. Though "officially" I was only 10 or 12 years older, he came to regard me as a father figure—or so his mother said once when thanking me for working with him.

When, four years later, Konrad married, I stood as his sponsor (the then equivalent of "best man") and in due course was asked to be godfather to his daughter. I declined, explaining that I was preparing to leave, having an offer to join the emperor in his fight against the Turks and would not be able to do my duty as godfather.

"Take me with you." Impossible of course, since I was going to be someone else by the time I got to Vienna.

"No. It is too dangerous. You have a family."

"I'm not afraid. You know I'm a good soldier."

"No, I do not. You do your exercises very well but you have never been in combat, which is completely different from breaking up a fight between a couple of drunks. In combat there are dozens of men flailing away around you and it's hard to tell friend from foe and coming out alive is as much luck as skill, probably more."

The Bishop gave me letter of introduction to a friend of his at the court in Vienna. "I said you had the most important qualification for command: you are lucky." I thanked him for his kindness and tucked it away, never to be used.

Konrad kept pestering me to take him. His wife visited me and begged me not to. She did not want to leave Paderborn or lose him. I reassured her.

Konrad tried one last time on the morning I left. "Why won't you take me?"

"Because I am a dangerous man. I always come out but many of those with me do not. My conscience is heavy with the widows and orphans of my enemies. I will not further burden it with the widows and orphans of my friends. I love you, Maria and Johanna too much to risk you."

I mention Konrad because some 20 years after leaving Paderborn I saw him again or, rather, he saw me. I was in Rome for the first time since the early years of the century and was sightseeing at the then new St. Peter's Basilica. I noticed a middle-aged man in uniform staring at and following me. He was with a priest. His curiosity finally got the best of him and he approached me, the priest looked confused.

"I am sorry to intrude but you look exactly like a man I knew a long time ago in Germany. He trained me to be a soldier." Eureka! Konrad. I did not recognize him as his body had thickened and his hair had thinned. He continued, "It's uncanny—face, hair, eyes, everything. Say, was your father's name Sebastian?" As he was speaking German, I could pretend not to understand and mumbled a few words in Italian. The priest spoke, in Italian, "I am Theodore von Wetzlar, Ambassador of the Archbishop-Elector of Cologne to the Holy See. This," indicating Konrad, "is the Captain of my guard." He then repeated what Konrad had said.

I forced a smile. "Ah, now I comprehend. I have a very ordinary face and it seems to have been a long time ago. Memory blurs."

"No!" Konrad was adamant. "I saw Sebastian every day for six years and I can still remember him perfectly." Several people had gathered around as Konrad was somewhat louder than normal conversation. As von Wetzlar was translating they strained to hear and those closer whispered to those further back. I loathe being the center of attention and snapped "I wasn't even born then. Yes, I may resemble this...this Sebastian, but obviously I am not he or related to him." As von Wetzlar translated, I pushed my way into the crowd. Konrad attempted to follow but von Wetzlar held him back.

I was shaken. Ever since my long entombment I knew my safety depended on always avoiding suspicion of...whatever—sorcery, deviance, heresy. Konrad also upset all my plans. I had just come to Rome planning on staying a few years and now I had to leave. Though Rome was much larger than when I was Octavian, I could not afford to meet Konrad again, and I was certain he would look for me. I took a boat to Naples the next morning.

A postscript: In 1650, Archbishop-Elector Ferdinand died and Paderborn was detached from his holdings to become an independent See under Prince-Bishop Dietrich von der Recke, who proved to be a progressive force in the Counter-Reformation. He also restored the city and cathedral after the damages of the Thirty Years' War. His tomb can be seen today in Paderborn Cathedral.

• •

THE FLOOD

"Après moi, le déluge," attributed to Louis XV of France, is often translated as "After me, the deluge" but more accurately as "After me, the flood." It is a matter of degree: While a deluge is a heavy rain, a flood sweeps away much of what is in its path. Such was the flood that overtook Louis XVI, the well-meaning, irresolute, and intellectually limited grandson and successor of Louis XV.

The winter of 1793 – 94 found me employed at the palace of a Baron Denis-Joseph Theriault to the southeast of Paris, near the town of Chaource, some 20 miles/30 kilometers south of Troyes in the province of Champagne. His holdings, as nearly as I can calculate from the 18th century measurements came to about 5,600 acres/2,200 hectares. In the Estates-General of 1789, Theriault has been a member of the Second Estate (nobles) and among the ultras. When a majority of the Second Estate had joined the Third (commoners) and a large portion of the First (clergy) to create the National Assembly, he withdrew and returned to his chateau.

That winter also saw the Reign of Terror and the most radical outbreaks of the Revolution. The guillotine frightened me. When the blade came down, a head tumbled into a basket and the trunk remained on the other side, either kneeling or tied to a plank. Would my head remain conscious if not connected to my body? I had always assumed, on no experience or evidence whatsoever that a sword would simply pass through my neck and leave no trace. But the blade of the guillotine stayed between the neck and the trunk.

Prior to joining Theriault I had been in Paris as a clerk with the *Ferme générale* which supervised and tabulated the revenues from the forty "tax farms" into which France was divided. Each farm was put up for auction every six years, the winner promising that amount to the Royal Treasury each of the six years with any excess collected, within a limit, paying the costs and profits to the "farmer." Working for the *Ferme générale* or one of the "farmers" was not a path to popularity. In 1790 when I had been there about three years the *Ferme générale* was abolished. Since the taxes and paperwork remained, most of the nearly 700 of us kept doing what we had been doing. *Plus ça change...*

My education, manner (and manners), and beliefs marked me as an aristocrat and Paris became uncomfortable after the execution of the king in January, 1793. Accordingly, gathering what I could carry on my horse—mostly gold coins, *Louis d'or*—and travelled to Troyes because I had made the acquaintance of, and done a favor for Augustin Sibille, the Constitutional Bishop of Aube, who had replaced the Bishop of Troyes when the latter refused to accept the Civil Constitution for the clergy. . I hoped he could point me to a position. He sent me to Theriault. Though on different sides of the revolution, Sibille and Theriault were on speaking terms. The Bishop warned me that the mood of the peasants was ugly and he thought that the days of the aristocracy were dwindling. Theriault took me on.

The estate had three overseers, one each for crops, wine, and livestock. As Theriault's accountant, I received their reports and kept the books for the estate. The unsettled times with many on the roads going to or running from something made it fairly easy to feed and I was there only seven months.

Theriault, in his early fifties with short-sighted blue eyes and brown hair turning white, while not fat did look prosperous. He rarely encountered the peasants except as he rode into or out of the estate when they were expected to stand, remove their hats and bow as he passed. Among his class he was neither among the best nor the worst. For a while he misjudged the temper of the times, believing that things would continue as they always had. The proclamation of a republic and execution of Louis XVI had disabused him of that notion.

In October, 1793, as news of disorders came in, he gathered what cash he had and sent his wife, two adult sons, their wives and children and his brother, also with an adult son, to the Austrian Netherlands (today's Belgium), some 120 miles/180 kilometers to the north. Joining with other fleeing aristocrats they were part of a caravan of over eighty persons, including about three dozen well-armed men.

By late February, 1794, toward the end of a harsh winter following a poor harvest, the tenants had exhausted their meagre stock of food and were asking Theriault to release more. He was torn between feeding his tenants and knowing that doing so would have to come from the feed for the livestock and the upcoming planting. Theriault distributed some and told the overseers to explain to the tenants that it was "hunger now or starvation next year." Hungry people are not amenable to logic; they need to eat now and will confront next year when it comes. The storm broke mid-morning on March 12. Boudreau, one of the overseers, burst into the palace yelling that the peasants were in revolt and a mob was marching to burn down the place and seize the livestock and food. Theriault asked, "How many?"

"Fifty or sixty," Boudreau answered, "some come from outside because they have heard we have food."

Theriault sighed. "Oh, let them have it, we are not enough to defend it and I do not want to kill anyone."

"I cannot say that about the mob," said Boudreau, "they killed Philippe," another overseer, "even though he was running away. I got away because they turned their attention to butchering the cattle which gives us time, but we had better clear out."

Theriault was resigned. "Where can we go? The forest is close but probably full of bandits. Think we can get to Troyes?"

I said, "Anything is better than getting lynched here."

"Get the servants," he ordered and I went to the landing and beat the gong until everyone in the house had assembled on the staircase from the ground floor.

Theriault spoke, "Anarchy has arrived. A mob will be here soon. Do not resist. They will probably burn down the house so take what you can, hide it if you can, and join the mob if you can. God be with you. Now go."

Some responded, "And with you." They scattered.

The Baron spoke to Boudreau and me, "Let's go. Grab a few things and meet at the stables in five minutes."

I ran upstairs to my room, stuffed some clothes into a pillow-case, picked up the strongbox with my emergency funds, and strapped on my rapier. I could now hear the mob drawing near. Another minute and they were in the house. Leaving my room, I saw men ascending the main staircase so I ran to the rear and found an empty staircase and ran down. As I got to the first landing one of the rebels stepped in front of me. We were both surprised. He was carrying a crude spear—a stick with a point —and before I could react he ran it into me. He looked up and his mouth opened, from fear or to scream. I thrust my sword under his chin and it penetrated through the base of his skull. Without a sound he went limp and dropped, sliding off my rapier. I pulled out the stick and as I turned the corner to go down, a group of four or five waving crude weapons, were rushing up towards me. I turned and ran up. When there was no up left I ran into a room and pushed an armoire against the door. I had barely time to look around the room when pounding on the door told me my pursuers had arrived. As I shoved a large chair against the armoire I heard "Burn him out!"

The room had a dormer window which I opened and crawled out to the roof. The slate roof was heavily pitched and I slid about ten feet until I was stopped by a slight rise at the edge. A face popped out of the window I had just exited and laughed, "Only one way to go, my Lord!" I looked over. There was no one on that side of the building, apparently everyone had come inside. As always, looking from the top appeared farther than being at the bottom looking up. I was reasonably, but not completely confident that I would survive the fall. I went over, bring my knees up to my chin and wrapping my arms around my legs, doing my best impression of a large ball. Then I was on the ground, no harm done. I ran, but no one chased me. I went to the Dower House, which had not yet been reached by the mob. Looking back, the chateau was on fire. The steward of the Dower House was standing at the front door staring at the burning building and I said, "A mob is looting the Chateau. Go and help yourself before everything is gone!" I went to the stables and was relieved to find two horses. I saddled one and rode off, leaving France and the Flood behind.

GOING HOME

1

Flames were all around us. After three months of marching, the bloodiest battle of Napoleon's entire career and the loss of almost half its men, la Grande Armée had finally reached Moscow, and the city was burning down. Men were chaotically rushing about trying to extinguish the flames and save enough of the city to billet the troops that remained.

We had crossed the Neman River with about 680,000 men and 200,000 horses. Drawn from France and a dozen subject states and forced allies like Austria and Prussia, it was the largest army that had ever assembled. Astride my horse on a small hillock, there were men, horses, artillery and wagons to the horizon. One of the most impressive sights I have ever seen. We looked unstoppable, but we stopped at Moscow because there was nowhere else to go except into the illimitable Russian steppes, which everyone from the Emperor to the lowliest private knew was the road to disaster. It was not the only road to that grim destination. The main portion of the army with Napoleon now numbered fewer than 100,000.

The day we arrived—14 September 1812—there were a few fires, but were thought sufficiently under control to allow us to occupy the city. Napoleon moved into the Kremlin to await a peace offer from Tsar Alexander I. The next day, large fires broke out and on the 16th threatened the Kremlin forcing Napoleon to flee the flames through the Arbat, which was almost totally destroyed. He went to a palace in the suburbs.

With the absence of the Emperor, the Army's discipline disintegrated and those Muscovites who remained were subjected to the horrors that have so often been inflicted by hungry, angry, frustrated armies. The most severe punishments only slowly restored some semblance of order.

After two days, the Emperor returned to the Kremlin and resumed waiting.

I was on the staff of General Armand de Caulaincourt, Duke of Vicenza in Napoleon's Kingdom of Italy, and Master of Horse to the Emperor, an office which encompassed much more than the name implied. He had been Ambassador to Russia and told Napoleon that Alexander would never negotiate while the French held Moscow. One of our duties was to investigate the fires and we found fuses all over the city that would have incinerated the buildings they were in had the flames reached them. We later learned that the Governor of Moscow, Count Rostopchin, had ordered the destruction of the city, making it part of the "scorched earth" strategy to deny food and shelter to the French.

The chaos made feeding very easy. At least the two times I needed prey that month. After midnight, I could walk the streets, look into half or more than half destroyed houses and either find someone inside or lure a scavenger inside with the offer of vodka. Covering the body with rubble, I could be confident that in the unlikely event the body was discovered, it would not provoke an investigation. There was simply too much else to do for what forces of law and order there were. Additionally, hunger and disease left bodies scattered around.

After a month, with the Russian winter coming on, realizing that Caulaincourt was right and Alexander would not negotiate, Napoleon evacuated Moscow. Our supply base was a thousand miles or more to the west, across land now largely barren and infested with guerillas, bandits, Cossacks, and pockets of Russian troops. We could not stay, we could not go on, we could only go home.

2

Thus began a storied disaster, a worthy complement to the Emperor's storied victories.

The Russian commander, Marshall Kutuzov, avoided a major engagement but was able to force us to go back the same way we came, through a devastated area denuded of food and shelter. We lost men every mile. Food was scarce, men and horses starved. The horses were eaten as they died, the cavalry marched just like the infantry. Then the snows came. And the cold. Men dropped and upon trying to rouse them one would be met with, "Go away. Let me sleep." The sleep was eternal.

Slogging through the snow brought the hunger on more often than less vigorous activities, every two or three weeks. Feeding was tricky, I could not bring my prey into a convenient hut. If a man wandered out of the line of march and fell in the snow, I would follow and go through a pantomime of trying to talk him back, the bend over and feed while pretending to try to lift him. I could do this only if I were there fairly quickly. The Russian winter did not take long to freeze the blood in the veins.

Another thing that did not take long was for comment to arise about my health in the midst of hunger and illness. A fellow officer once asked, "Really, Leblanc, how do you do it? The rest of us are walking bushes and you look like you just came from a barber." After that I made a show every morning of rubbing snow on my face and scrapping it with my razor. Since the snow raised gooseflesh others who tried it did not try it often.

Once, going through the performance of helping a fallen soldier, I heard sounds behind me, and turning saw a pack of wolves coming at me. Snow was falling but not thickly enough to obscure me from the soldiers trudging past, not more than 120 yards away. I did not have time to run back to the line and my flintlock pistol had only one shot, not that I was certain it was loaded. Even I could not explain away surviving such an attack. All this passed through my mind in less time than it takes to tell and now the wolves were nearly upon me. Then they stopped and fell quiet. Did they recognize me as one of their own, a predator like them? I stood and backed away toward the soldiers and after a few yards turned and ran as fast as I could through the snow to the line. As I reached the others, everyone backed away from me.

"Do I smell that bad? Even the wolves will not get near me." I laughed but no one else did, or said a word to me.

The wolves were tearing at the man I had left behind.

Later, that evening, when I had rejoined my unit, General Caulaincourt took me aside, "I hear that you put on quite a show this afternoon, staring down a pack of ravenous wolves. The men do not know whether to applaud you or burn you at the stake."

I liked that explanation. It was better than anything I had thought to say. "It surprised me. Maybe the wolves thought I was dead and were disoriented when I stood. I do not want to try to do it again!"

"Seriously, Captain, I get questions about you. Why you never lose weight even though you eat practically nothing, or seem to get tired, or that the cold and wind do not bring color to your cheeks." He gave a short, forced laugh, "They want me to check if you are human."

I was not going to answer that, but I did say, "I have never been a heavy eater. I do get tired but try not to show it as an example to the men. And I bundle up against the cold and wind. Luckily, I am just a healthy man."

"Certainly that is the logical explanation, but the men are susceptible to superstitious fantasies. Please be careful, I do not want someone testing your humanity by taking a shot at you."

In my mind's ear there rose the voice of Josef saying almost the same thing so many centuries before.

And so it went as we trudged back to the Neman. At the end of November, crossing the Berezina River, we were attacked by a large Russian army. We were sitting ducks, trying to cross on a three narrow improvised bridges and lost probably between a third and half of our remaining men—we could no longer be called an army.

Shortly after that, Napoleon received news that there had been an attempted coup in Paris and departed as fast as he could, leaving Murat in command.

On December 14 the last of the *Grande Armée* left Russia. Perhaps 30,000 men. The others had been killed, captured, died in the retreat, deserted, and some few groups found their way out by other routes.

The spell that Napoleon had cast on Europe for fifteen years was broken. The allies broke ranks, first Prussia, whose commander, General Yorck, signed a convention with the Russians on December 30 and joined the Russians. At first disowned by his king, he now stands as one of Germany's great heroes and an example of principled disobedience to orders; a pity that more did not copy him. Soon Prussia was followed by Austria and then the smaller states. While Napoleon was attempting to rebuild the French Army, his former allies joined with England in the Sixth Coalition and in the following October, at the Battle of Leipzig, destroyed Napoleon's empire. He abdicated, becoming Emperor of Elba, made a quixotic attempt at a restoration, which Europe would never have allowed, that ended at Waterloo, still the preferred word for complete and irretrievable defeat.

I wish to end this episode with a few words about a man I esteem, General Caulaincourt. He always resented that Bonaparte had used him as a cat's-paw in the murder of the Duke d'Enghien but nonetheless served him to the end, one of the few around the Emperor who would speak truth to him and becoming Foreign Minister during the Hundred Days, tried vainly to convince the rest of Europe of Napoleon's peaceful intentions. After Waterloo, Caulaincourt was proscribed at the Restoration, faced a death sentence, and was freed only upon the intercession of Tsar Alexander. In retirement, Caulaincourt wrote *With Napoleon in Russia*, not published until a century after his death and, to me, the definitive work on the tragedy. During the Second World War, it was read by German generals in Russia. They could not have found much comfort there.

VERONICA

1

Eighteen-seventy-one found me in New York City I had come to the United States for the first time 10 years before, to participate in the War Between the States. I arrived in Boston as an Italian veteran of Garibaldi's march. I obtained the name and papers from one of my prey in Naples shortly after the collapse of the Bourbon monarchy and the incorporation of the Kingdom of the Two Sicilys into the new Kingdom of Italy. Garibaldi was an international hero, no place more than the United States because of his support of the Union anti-slavery cause. When I arrived in Boston in December, 1861 and went to the army recruiting center, my credentials got me an immediate commission as Captain of a company of volunteers.

It is often difficult to distinguish one battle from another except through changes in weaponry. The United States Civil War was the first in which I participated that had repeating rifles, which greatly increased the firepower of the forces. At the beginning of the war the Quartermaster Corps did not order many because of the fear that the soldiers would waste bullets by firing blindly until the magazine was empty. Single-shot bolt action rifles were gradually replaced as the war dragged on and bullets could be manufactured by millions. That is by way of an introduction to the Battle of Fredericksburg in December, 1862. The commander of the Army of the Potomac, Major General Ambrose Burnside, planned a rapid crossing of the Rappahannock River, turn south and get to Richmond behind Lee and the Army of Northern Virginia. As happens too often, bureaucratic dilatoriness held up delivery of the pontoon bridges long enough for Lee to double back and to build a strong defensive position opposite us. I was a company commander in Major General George Meade's division when it tried to outflank the Confederate left at Marye's Heights and ran into heavy artillery fire and several thousand well positioned Confederates. The rapid fire rifles were telling. Our battalion, and my company, were cut to pieces. Amid the cries and screams of the wounded I was wondering how I could get back because my uniform had at least six bullet holes—well beyond my capacity to explain. As the fighting moved away from our sector, I finally decided just to take off my jacket and shirt and make my way back. As I was removing them, a badly wounded man a couple of yards away stared at me and tried to speak but only was able choke on his blood, tried to raise his hand but could not. He was shivering so I put my jacket on him, bending close, held his hand saying softly "Do not be afraid. Soon you too shall rise again." He gave my hand a weak squeeze and tried to smile as I moved off. For those few seconds I was more of a priest than I had ever been when I was a priest.

Getting back to our lines, I ran the last hundred or so yards waving my Union cap and yelling "Union! Union!" My clothing, or lack thereof, caused much comment; it was, after all, December. My jacket went to cover a cold, wounded soldier (true) and my shirt caught on a bush and it was faster to take it off than to disentangle it (not true). Do not be overly impressed with how quickly I came up with that lie. I had used it previously in similar circumstances.

There was some muttering on a variation of "I've never seen

so many Reb sharpshooters miss so easy a target." I was nick-named "Lucky" for the remainder of the war—partly because it was easier to pronounce than my Italian name.

After that, as usual, I came through the war with several more seemingly inexplicably narrow escapes from death. I rose to brevet Lieutenant-Colonel, commanding a battalion and was honorably discharged. Of all my wars, the highest rank I ever attained. Returning to Boston a minor celebrity, I accepted one of the positions offered, as international correspondent for a large shipping line. Considering how hard I had to work to learn languages, I was happy to be able to turn a profit on them.

In 1869, cashing in my savings, I accompanied one of the shipments to Hamburg, then an independent city in the North German Confederation, settled a misunderstanding and accounts with our agent there, told him I wanted to see Paris and vanished into a new identity. I could have spent a few more years in Boston before my face betrayed me, but I was restless and, while Boston was a delightful place, it was much smaller than the cities I preferred. I would meet companions from the war who would talk loud and long about my luck in the battles. Also, there had been speculation in the newspapers about the disappearance of young men of the lower classes.

Once in Hamburg I set out to find the next Sebastian. Hamburg was an embarkation port for emigrants to the United States and I had a wide choice of young men who were travelling alone. The combination of a hot meal, beer, and companionship loosened tongues and brought forth the information I needed: Foremost, whether someone was waiting for them in New York. A surprising number were making the voyage on hope alone, relying on the *turnvereins* and *bunds* in the United States to assist them in getting employment and learning English. Making my selection, a man of 21 who had his papers and a working ticket on a just docked freighter departing five days hence, I laid out my plans. Saying I was travelling on the same

ship, I contrived to encounter him twice in the next three days
—loneliness, as I keep saying, is my greatest ally—and on the
third evening suggested we go to the port to look at the ship.
Having nothing better, or even anything else to do, he agreed. I
had reconnoitered and had found a close to ideal setting: a vacant building between a side street and alley. The lock on the
front door was broken and the back door opened on to the alley.
It was about nine and dark on a late September evening. Everything went as I had rehearsed. Passing the door I pretended to
trip, pushing against him forcing him into and through the door,
landing on top of him, and kicking the door shut. The blade
was already in my hand and immediately at his jugular. I fed,
cleaned up, removed his coat and papers, and dragged the body
into the unlit alley, expecting the rats to mutilate it so the
method of death would not be apparent.

2

About two weeks later I disembarked in New York, one of
the few times I have used the same country twice in succession.
The voyage was uneventful, I was working for food and passage, but the duties were lighter than expected: The stevedores
in New York made it plain they did not need my help. Im-
migration was a simple routine—this was before Ellis Island—I
looked healthy, spoke English, and had money.

Moving money under different names required some planning. As I said, I took my money from Boston to Hamburg and
after obtaining my new identity, purchased a letter of credit
from a Hamburg bank, keeping enough cash to see me through
the first few weeks. This episode revolves around money so let's
establish a standard. As nearly as I can tell from the statistics,
an 1871 dollar had the purchasing power of almost $30 in 2018.
That mere statistic is, however, misleading. In the 1870's, a salary of $20 a week allowed a fairly comfortable life for a family
of three or four. Today, $600 a week would barely keep a single
person sheltered and fed in New York. The difference is the

range of what one purchased. In 1871, the $20 would secure the necessities: rent, food, clothes, and occasional luxuries like a show or dining out. The list of "necessities" has expanded somewhat since. There were virtually no taxes or social security to deduct from your salary. When not walking, transportation was a horse-drawn bus that cost a nickel to go from 14th Street to Central Park, considered "a day in the country". Only the wealthy owned carriages and kept horses.

Leaving the dock, I secured a room on 7th Street, between First and Second Avenues. In those days (you will notice that sometimes I talk like an old man) 14th Street was the center of middle class New York, a bustling, colorful neighborhood. The city was expanding rapidly northward, particularly for the upper-middle and upper classes.

While the money I transferred from the letter of credit to open a bank account in New York would be sufficient for several months, I still needed to find employment. The demand for mercenary soldiers had evaporated in the countries I wanted to inhabit. The telegraph and trans-Atlantic cable meant that I could no longer claim experience or education because it had become was too easy to check my references. Existence was getting more and more complicated.

Languages had proven to be my most marketable skill to prospective employers. I was now fluent in five—English, French. Italian, German, and Spanish, but sometimes lapsing into archaic words or grammar; Latin and Greek I maintained as they bespoke a classical education which afforded social entrée. I was hired full-time by a law firm representing European companies here and arranging for representation of American companies in Europe. I later learned that three part-time translators had been fired because I could do all of the work more cheaply.

I found an ideal "dining room," a small space in a warehouse near the Bowery docks with a dirt floor. Preparing and maintaining that room was, and is, an enormous task, probably beyond a man who tires or would become sore. This room was about 12 feet by 16 feet so I could fit ten 3 feet by 6 feet graves; at eight feet deep I could stack three bodies in each. Thirty meals, a little more than two years. A lot of digging and not something I can hire others to do. I finished an even smaller side room and furnished it as a sitting room and stocked it with liquor. I wanted my guests to feel comfortable.

About eight months after my arrival, one of the attorneys invited me to join the stag line at a cotillion, a coming-out affair for young ladies of the "better sort". In reality, the parents were putting their wares on display for prospective marriages. Not being in or on the market, I could enjoy myself without calculating my chances with this or that heiress. After several dances, the orchestra took a rest and I was with a few acquaintances around the bar. One drew our attention to a very plain young lady sitting next to an older, more attractive woman.

"That's the Strang girl and her mother. I bet she hasn't had one dance. Even all her father's money isn't enough to interest anyone in her."

"On top of being ugly, she really is a half-wit, maybe less than half," said another.

A third, more sympathetic, said, "She was born soft in the head. My mother says it was because her mother was over 40 and had no business having a child."

"Look at the way she's dressed. I've seen nuns in more daring clothes. She's hiding all her...er...charms."

"You can't hide what you don't have."

While they wer laughing over their petty cruelties, my mind was buzzing, calculating away, and had been since the magical phrase "all her father's money." I had put myself on the market.

A wealthy young lady with no prospects was ideal. Even after centuries I hated hustling after jobs and money.

The orchestra was returning. I excused myself and walked over to the pair.

"Good evening, I'm Sebastian Smith," bowing slightly to each in turn. The mother was tight-lipped but the girl glanced up quickly then looked down at her hands, holding a small bouquet. "I...I...I'm Veronica." Stammered so softly that I barely heard above the noise of the room.

"A pleasure to meet you. May I have the honor of this dance?"

"I...I...I don't dance very good," she raised her eyes but not her head.

"That's all right. Neither do I. We just take two steps to the right, then two to the left, and then do it again and again until the music stops." I smiled. She looked pleased, a smile without showing her teeth.

"Can I, mummy?" Both diffident and pleading.

Her mother was obviously torn between protecting Veronica from humiliation and letting her join in the fun that everyone else seemed to be enjoying. She looked at me as if trying to read my intentions. I hoped I was showing a puppy-like friendliness.

"Yes." Said with more doubt than enthusiasm, but it was yes.

When I placed my left hand on the middle of her back, I felt her flinch. I relaxed and let her decide how close to dance. We could have fit her mother between us. She started awkwardly but after a couple of minutes got into the simple rhythm of our dance. As I brought her back to her seat after the dance she had a real smile, teeth and all.

"Oh, mummy, that was so much fun."

Her mother inclined slightly toward me, "Thank you, Mr.

Smith."

I bent toward Veronica, "The evening is young, perhaps you will favor me again." I walked toward another of the young ladies.

I danced twice more with Veronica, as many times as with anyone. She moved closer, though not touching, each time.

There came a point where the young men were invited to dance with the chaperones. I made certain I got to Mrs. Strang.

After a few steps she said, "My, Mr. Smith..."

"Please call me Sebastian."

"As you wish. I was going to say that you are quite a good dancer despite what you told Veronica."

"I am spurred to greater heights by an excellent partner."

"You are shameless." She gave a little laugh.

More seriously, she asked, "Why did you dance with Veronica?"

"The first time because she was not dancing and I felt it was my duty as a stag. The second time was because I wished to, as will be the next."

"Then why the second time? I am sadly aware of my daughter's shortcomings and I was very reluctant to bring her here and expose her to the mocking that she has too often had to endure." A slight pause, "So why?"

"I am taken by how much joy she found in that simple two-step. You saw her smile. Such simple, pure innocence is very rare in these jaded times."

"It is that simple innocence that so worries her father and me. It would be so easy for someone to take advantage of her." Was this a warning that she knew what I was up to, or just the normal defensiveness of a mother with a vulnerable child?

With deference to the young men dancing with older women, this was the shortest dance of the evening. I escorted her back to Veronica, from whom I extracted, with very little effort, a promise for the last dance.

After the dance, as I accompanied them to the cabs, I handed Veronica my card, which Mrs. Strang took, as I said "I hope to see you again." I helped Veronica into the cab and turned to her mother who said "Thank you so much, Mr....uh...Sebastian. Good night."

I thought it likely that I had made a start on her sympathy and would see Veronica again.

<h3 style="text-align:center">3</h3>

"Again" came less than three weeks later when I received an invitation to dinner at the Strang's, evening wear. While waiting for the invitation, which I was almost certain would come, I had done some research on Andrew Strang and, no, I had not forgotten my previous encounter with an Andrew. The son of an immigrant from what is now Belgium fleeing the Napoleonic Wars, he was 63. As a child he went to work in a textile mill, where children were wanted because their small, nimble fingers could reach into the spindles and retie broken thread, a constant problem. The child showed a considerable aptitude for machinery and learned to repair machines. In his early 20's he opened his own repair shop and soon designed improved machines. With financial backing he was able to open a manufacturing company and when his backers sold out in 1869, Mr. Strang's share was reported as $1,800,000, a considerable fortune for the day. Acutely aware of his lack of education, he was relentlessly self-improving. Proud of his excellent library, he was quick to point out that he had read most of the books there. On day, in the library which had full shelves and books piled on tables, he joked, "I don't remember buying that many. I think they breed when my back is turned."

When I arrived, Mr. Strang opened the door himself explaining "The butler is serving drinks which is, of course, much more important than opening doors." Introducing myself and shaking hands, he added, "Mary told me of your kindness to Veronica, who came home very happy. Thank you." I had the wind at my back.

The dinner was family. Veronica had a brother, Robert, who looked to be about 27 or 28, nearly ten years older than his sister. Robert had married a few months previously, to the daughter of one of "the 400." Her parents, Mr. and Mrs. Winslow also were there, hence the evening dress. Upon longer acquaintance with Andrew Strang, he made plain his contempt for "that ass, McAllister and the snobs who follow him" but because the children have to make their way with them, "I go along with the tomfoolery."

Anticipating questions about my background, I had put together a story to cover both my education and reason for being in the United States. I had written it out for later reference so as to keep the story consistent over time. I can attest to the truth of Mark Twain's adage that no one has a good enough memory to be a successful liar. This story was that I had been born in Hannover in 1848, the youngest of three sons and two daughters of a middle official in the government of the Kingdom of Hannover, incorporated into Prussia after the Austro-Prussian Seven Weeks' War in 1866. The King of Hannover, George V, was a first cousin to Queen Victoria, who may have wanted to aid him but her Prime Minister, the Whig Earl of Derby, was having no part of the quarrels in Germany. Upon the abolition of the kingdom, my father lost his position, having been outspokenly anti-Prussian. When I completed my *Abitur*, there was no money for university; my father gave me what he could and recommended that I leave Germany. "And here I am." Veronica thought my story "the most romantic thing I have ever heard."

"I don't think losing your position and having to leave your home is all that romantic." Robert smilingly chided.

"But then I would not be enjoying the pleasure of this excellent company."

Mrs. Strang gave a little laugh and when I looked at her, winked at me. Was she on to me?

Mrs. Winslow said, approvingly, "Those are the manners Mr. McAllister is trying to teach us."

Mr. Strang gave a low snort but said nothing.

Since he has now twice intruded into our story, a few words about Ward McAllister. A *soi-disant* southern gentleman, he came to New York and set himself up as the arbiter of society. His goal in the last half of the 19th century was to bring a higher level of snobbery to New York and found among the *nouveau riche* willing students, including using French when perfectly adequate English terms—"self-styled" and "newly rich"—were available. He coined the term "the 400" and urged the wealthy to emulate the English aristocracy. In the early 1890's he overstepped and wrote a kind of memoir in which he dropped every name he could remember. The result, among the 400, who loathed what they considered cheap publicity, was that he was spurned and ostracized for the rest of his life. Truman Capote could have spared himself much anguish had he paid attention to McAllister's fate.

4

Over the next nearly a year I would take Veronica on dates, generally to plays, concerts, or revues that she enjoyed because she did not have to interact with many people, which, realizing she had been given less than the others, caused her to be nervous and unhappy. On nice weekends we would have picnics in Central Park. She loved those.

When I brought Veronica home after a New Year's Eve show early in the morning of January 1, 1873, Mr. Strang asked if he might call upon me that afternoon when we had had some sleep. I agreed. This was what I had been working toward.

Promptly at two the doorbell rang. I admitted Mr. Strang and brought him into my apartment of a sitting room, bedroom, and semi-private bath located between my apartment and my neighbor's.

"No kitchen?"

"I dine out."

"Easier than cooking."

"Not always." Damn! The mouth is faster than the brain.

"I know what you mean. You can't always get exactly what you want the way you want it."
I beamed upon him. "Precisely."

We sat.

"I'm sure you know that Veronica is in love with you. You are almost the only person outside of the family who treats her as an equal. Her mother and I are very grateful for that, even if it is only your good manners."

"It goes deeper than that."

"What are your intentions?" He gave a rueful laugh, "I sound like I'm in a bad melodrama."

"There are not many other ways to ask that question. I love Veronica, but am in no position to give her the life she deserves. I make a decent living for one person and, by being careful, am able to move in social circles above my means. I cannot support a wife and family comfortably."

"Those are the two things I have come to discuss. First, as

to having a family, Veronica may not be able to have children. Frankly, man to man, she has not had the change of body that girls go through. She is also extremely bashful, so much so that you would probably need to have separate bedrooms. You have noticed, I'm certain, that she always wears dresses that go up to her chin and with long sleeves. She does not even let her mother see her unless she is fully dressed. Even if she can, she certainly should not have children, her nerves are too fragile and she would not be able to cope with children even with maids and nannies. If a family is in your plans, you will need to break off with Veronica. Better the heartbreak now than later."

Perfect. Trying to act embarrassed, but not able to blush, I stammered "That...that is not a problem."

"Are you sure?"

I paused to give the impression that what I was about to say was painful and came reluctantly. "Because you have been honest with me, I will be the same with you," said with a perfectly straight face. "A severe case of mumps" which I gave the German pronunciation of *moomps*, "a few years ago makes it unlikely that I can have children."

Mr. Strang could almost conceal his pleasure. He was able to say "Oh. That's too bad," with more sympathy than he probably felt.

A short, awkward silence ensued which I broke.

"You said, sir, that you had two things to discuss. Is the other still relevant?"

"More relevant than ever." He was no longer making an effort to conceal his pleasure. "As you can imagine, her mother and I worry constantly about Veronica. We are both past 60 and need to provide for her future. We do not want her to be institutionalized and feel it would be unfair to Robert to make him responsible for her as well as his own family, though he would be willing." A pause. I knew what he was about to say but he was trying to phrase it with more delicacy than I needed. I raised my eyebrows looking expectant and inviting him to continue. After a couple of minutes he said "I know this may sound crass, but I am prepared to give Veronica a comfortable dowry upon her marriage to the right man. Unless my judgment has completely deserted me, you are that man."

I win.

Veronica was not the first heiress I pursued, but was the first I caught. Families were wary of young men, immigrants without antecedents or prospects, however cultured, polite, or well-educated. Or they wanted children. For Veronica's parents that was secondary to providing for her security. Everything came together for me. With enough time, anything that can happen, will.

We were married in a small, family-only ceremony at Trinity Church in April, 1873. Her parents gave us a small townhouse on 16th street, just to the east of Third Avenue. The house was new and very up-to-date, even a real bathroom with a flush toilet. If you have never had to go to an outhouse in January or use or smell or empty a chamber pot, you will never fully appreciate the luxury that is indoor plumbing. We found a widow and her daughter as cook and housekeeper. It was inconvenient to have to eat meals regularly. It strengthened my appreciation of indoor plumbing.

Upon marriage, I left my job but, not wishing to become part of the idle rich, I looked for something to do. Robert, who worked in his father-in-law's small investment house, suggested that I could come there, unsalaried, and learn the business. Basically, I was a very early intern. Mr. Winslow liked the idea, agreeing to my condition that no one be fired.

I settled into the boring but not unpleasant life of the upper middle class. Within two months of my joining the firm, the Panic of 1873 hit—not cause and effect. In September, Jay Cooke, one of the most prominent houses, went into bankruptcy. The ripples spread and the next few years were the "Great Depression" until replaced by that of the 1930's. By January the decline in business activity affected J. S. Winslow & Co. Andrew Strang's conservative investments, largely United States bonds and United Kingdom consols, were largely unaffected so Robert and I were able to deposit securities in the firm and become junior partners. We rode out the crisis.

Veronica was an undemanding spouse, cheerfully accepting that occasionally I had undefined "man things" to do, which covered my hunting. Having separate bedrooms was a real convenience because she never knew how late I came home. She slept soundly nine or ten hours a night. A perfect wife in every way save intellect. No snide remarks. Intelligent conversation is one of life's great pleasures.

Our life was a narrow circle of friends and we saw quite a lot of Veronica's parents. When Mr. Strang died in 1881, Mrs. Strang told me that Andrew and she thought I was the best decision they ever made, Veronica was happy and secure, their worries were gone and then she thanked me. I felt that my existence was almost justified.

By the time Mrs. Strang followed her husband in 1885, I was having to consider my departure, particularly how to be certain Veronica would continue to be secure.

5

A brief aside to reminisce about one of the most remarkable phenomena of my long existence: The telephone. Invented in 1876, the first exchange in New York City came in 1880. Within five years, telephone wires spread like supernatural vines from pole to pole and building to building throughout the city. Except that the great blizzard of 1888 knocked down so many of the wires, leading to their burial under the streets, the wires would have blotted out the sky.

The first time I used a telephone I was stunned. Standing in the office and speaking with a man half a mile away appeared to me the apex of human achievement. It was, as it turned out, only the beginning. I witnessed a repeat in this century when cell phones seemed to spring spontaneously in every human hand.

6

Eighteen eighty-seven and time to move on. I had spent more time in New York than anyplace since I left Mathilde, not counting the 182 years spent in Hell, as I always regarded my burial. I was getting comments on how young I looked while Veronica was settling into matron hood and Robert middle-age. I would pass it off by saying it was because Veronica took such good care of me, which greatly pleased her, causing her to giggle like a little girl. Unlike the past, I could not just disappear, which would be unfair, even cruel to Veronica. Somehow I had to kill this Sebastian off so that it was known he was dead, she could have some closure, and not spend a lifetime and fortune trying to find me, for she was that kind of romantic.

I had been preparing for this since our marriage. I was moving money to a private account that I could access under another name, from another place, while preserving enough to take care of Veronica after I was gone. I had, a few years prior, set up a lifetime trust for her "care and comfort" into which I made a large initial, and thereafter regular contributions. It was, I felt, now sufficient. I also had a will, with Robert as executor, as I was executor for his; women, it was felt, could not be trusted or burdened or any of a dozen other excuses with such a responsibility. He was also residual legatee, or his children if he predeceased Veronica. Having worked at a law office had been quite useful in augmenting my legal jargon.

I needed a body, rarely a problem. I needed a location, more of a problem. Unlike the dining rooms it had to be a neighborhood in which I could plausibly be found. The tricky part was, I needed a building that would be vacant, but might be inhabited, perhaps by squatters. I wanted only to burn one body beyond recognition, not a building's worth. I regularly used my lunch hour to walk around lower Manhattan near the docks, where the office was.

Because of my reaction to food, I went to lunch only when business required. Victorians of the upper class, with whom I associated, ate beyond the imagination of today's diners. Lunch would be four or five courses and, a few hours later, dinner, seven or eight; wine, beer, and whisky flowing. At five-feet-ten and about 160 pounds, I was considered practically emaciated. That I walked an hour for exercise was regarded as a bizarre eccentricity. Needless to say, they died off in droves in their 50's and 60's from apoplexy, a portmanteau covering any sudden death such as heart attacks, strokes or aneurysms.

In New York, then as now, if one looked long enough, one could find anything. Eventually I came across an empty three-family row house off Canal Street. The back had a wood staircase with a small porch on each floor which had a back door that could be opened by a simple skeleton key. The interior was very dusty and, except for a few small tables and chairs, unfurnished, apparently unoccupied for some time. It was probably a casualty of the depression, unable to be maintained or sold. Now for the body. Having only an hour restricted my search, and I had to check nearly every day that the house was still empty, also to put it in a state to serve my plan. I also had to find someone of about my build. I looked among the immigrants who disembarked almost daily. I will not bore you with my hours of failures, but in the third week I got lucky. I found a despondent young man standing next to a carpet valise, holding a crudely lettered sign saying "Hungry. Will Work." He did not speak English, knew no one, and was overjoyed that I spoke Italian and had a job to offer. On my asking, he said the sign had been written by someone he met on the boat who then went off with family. He was not really hungry, he had brought a few dollars with him. I told him that "hungry" had attracted my notice which is why his acquaintance had written it. I explained that I had just purchased an old house and needed help to make it livable and would pay him three dollars a day, plus lunch and he could stay there until he found lodging. He picked up the valise and we walked to the house.

The house we entered was more cluttered than I had found it. I had regularly added papers and other flammables. I brought Gianni to the second floor. He talked about how bad things were in Lucania, the poor soil that grew little, "the poorest part of a poor country." He also said that he had done a lot of work around the farm where his father was a tenant, and he was sure I would be satisfied with him. Altogether a pleasant young man. Such is the price of necessity. After a few minutes, when I asked about removing the badly torn wallpaper, he turned to look and I struck him as hard as I could on the back of the head with a lead pipe I had concealed under papers on a table. He went down without a sound.

Do you have any idea how difficult it is to undress and dress an inert human body? Neither did I. I pulled on his clothes and the body followed. I secured the body and pulled, tugged, twisted and wrestled, finally having all of his clothes in a pile. I changed into them and then tugged, twisted, tucked until I got my clothes on him. Taking a last look at my watch before consigning it to the flames, I found I had spent almost an hour-and-a-half. Already the office must have wondered what happened as I was noted for my punctuality. I also checked his pulse, I wanted to be certain he was dead before the fire. I do what I must but try not to inflict pain.

As I was about to light the fire, I noticed the valise and

brought it with me. I wanted as few anomalies as possible for the inspectors. I lit a fire on the second floor, ran down and started another on the first and walked around to the front. I went around the corner and waited. A minute or two passed before the flames became visible and a few more before someone ran to the fire bell. By the time, several minutes later, the fire brigade arrived, the building was collapsing. I left my semi-concealment and walked by. A large crowd had gathered. I said, in a very heavy accent, to one man at the back of the crowd, but loudly enough for those nearby to hear "Someone cried there was a child and a man ran in." He turned to talk with others and I left, confident that the story of the child would get to the police and that Veronica's husband had died a hero.

The evening papers carried the story, saying that at press time the building was not safe enough to inspect. The morning papers reported that a body had been found. That evening, Sebastian Smith had been identified by the inscription on his watch and was acclaimed a hero, though no child had been found. Several "eyewitnesses" had heard the cry and seen him rush into the building—just as I expected.

7

A few months previously, I had acquired the papers for a new identity. For the first time I was an American. I had rented a room further north and west, on 22nd street, between 8th and 9th where I could spend a few days undetected until I booked passage to my next home. And tidied up—I had the last of my dining room cellars paved. Having spent sixteen years in New York, I left behind six crypts. I have often wondered, as New York was built, rebuilt, and re-rebuilt, what the excavators made of those neat arrays of bones. Perhaps in their haste, they did not even notice.

I found a ship stopping at Rio de Janeiro and then Buenos Aires. I was tempted by Rio, largely because Brazil was a constitutional monarchy and I remained a monarchist at heart. It was regarded as the most stable and best-governed country in Latin America. However, it also meant learning Portuguese.

Six days later I left New York, not to return for nearly ninety years.

Two years after my arrival the monarchy was abolished. Emperor Pedro II, old, tired, and without an heir, went into a not unwilling exile, and Brazil became just another unstable republic subject to coups and corruption. I did not stay long, though I have been back and do enjoy the city and the *cariocas*.

Investing wisely or luckily, I still live off of Veronica's dowry. Among my regrets is that I do not know how she fared after my "death." One of the banes of my existence is that it is full of loose threads and unfinished stories. Another of the frustrations is not being able to finish things. I console myself that I gave Veronica fourteen happy, contented years and hope they were not the best of her life.

THE GREAT WAR

1

By 1912 it was time to move on. I had spent several years living once again in Rome, which I returned to at periods sufficiently lengthy to preclude being recognized by anyone from a previous stay. That sojourn had been as a Viennese. It is always convenient to live as an alien in a country. It explains any lapse in knowledge of custom, language, and geography as well as the absence of relatives and childhood or school friends. Possessed of the identity and papers of a young Italian who was a graduate of the University of Naples and had recently completed his military service as a Lieutenant in the army reserve—excellent credentials--I went to Paris, another haunt (you will pardon the expression) to which I regularly return. In 1912 it required no more than a train ticket for me to cross national borders. Passports and border checks were almost unknown.

Of my thousand years, *La Belle Époque*--1890 to 1914—is my favorite. The most important "modern conveniences" had appeared: electricity, indoor plumbing, trains, and, after the turn of the century, automobiles, which became and remain a passion of mine. As always, it did take a certain income level to enjoy fully the glories of the time. This I had. The gold standard, to which the majority of the European world adhered, kept prices stable and money valuable.

In those years, many young men and fewer young women came to Paris—aspiring artists, largely painters and musicians, most with more hope than talent. They were people with no family or connections and few friends in the city. It was easy to make acquaintances and a meal would induce trust. When I needed to feed, it was easy to find prey. Occasionally a body was found in the Seine and generally was ascribed to robbery by "Apaches." There must have been wonderment as to why anyone would rob an archetypal "starving artist."

2

The Great War— always and ever it will be that. Most of the tragedies of the twentieth century—World War II, Hitler, Stalin and beyond--resulted directly from the decisions made during and after the war. Even as I write, the Middle East is saturated with blood because of what statesmen pleased to call themselves "peacemakers" were equally pleased to call a "settlement" in the aftermath of the Great War.

When World War I broke out at the beginning of August, 1914, it was widely anticipated that the troops would be "home for Christmas." The Germans expected that their great sweep through Belgium and northern France would encircle the French army and force capitulation. Equally, the French were certain that their overwhelming thrust into Alsace-Lorraine would carry them all the way to Berlin. In proof of Moltke's dictum that when war begins, all plans are obsolete, both attacks failed with massive casualties. By Christmas, the western front had already settled into the trenches that ran from the English Channel to the Swiss border, as it remained for more than three years, during which hundreds of meters were bought and sold with thousands of lives.

One would think that the unexpected, unprecedented bloodletting would have given men reason to find a way out, back to a peace that however imperfect, would be better than the war. Yet the dead, under some form of "they must not have died in vain" became themselves the excuse for continuing the killing. Tragedy begets tragedy and ever more tragedy.

Italy was neutral for nearly the first year of the war. I volunteered for the French army and, on the basis of my degree and the papers showing my military training and reserve commission, and convincing the army board that, though a foreigner I was eager to fight for France, I was accepted as a lieutenant. Because of my languages, I was originally assigned to Intelligence, which was against my wishes. Naturally, I wanted to be in the front lines. That is where the blood is. As you know by now, I have no compunction about killing to feed, but if men are inclined send their young men to butcher one other for my benefit, so much the better.

I began the war as liaison to English units and interrogating German prisoners. However, casualties among company officers—lieutenants and captains—were extremely heavy and by November my request for a transfer was approved and I was on the front line near Amiens as a Company commander with the rank of Captain. The war was beginning to settle into the trench stalemate that would characterize the Western Front. At this point the front, including the trenches, were rather haphazard. While I had to be careful, it was not difficult to feed on a wounded man in a shell hole during a battle while everyone else was too busy trying to stay alive to pay attention to me.

In the spring of 1915, my company ran into particularly heavy, and accurate, fire. I noticed several holes in my uniform. Usually, I would simply take it off and say that I was caught on the wire. This time there were too many men around to try that and I had to roll in the mud (always available) to cover the holes A spare uniform was not available in the trench. The mud got me through the next day, but the day after that a heavy rain fell cleaning my uniform sufficiently for the holes to appear. Before

I could do anything about it, one of the NCO's coming behind me said he saw holes in the back of my jacket. He came around to the front and when he saw the holes there his expression was a mixture of disbelief, wonder, and, though I may have interpreted wrongly, fear.

"You have bullet holes."

"They just tore my clothes. I was lucky."

"It looks like the shots went right through you."

"I guess I was too cold and tired to notice." I laughed. "As you see, I am alive and well."

He laughed, nervously. I relied on the solid common sense of the stolid French soldier to believe what was in front of him and stay away from the supernatural.

Though I tried to be careful not to expose myself needlessly to fire, as the weeks passed more comments expressed incredulity at my luck. The men tended to stay close, hoping my luck would also protect them—which not only failed but severely crimped my feeding. I never want an audience. There were not many full-scale "over the top" battles, but there were more or less constant skirmishes, snipers and always the artillery. In May, a shell scored a direct hit in my section of the trench. Of the eight or nine men, I was the only one to crawl out, my clothes torn and covered with blood--other men's--but I did not have a scratch on me. Despite my protests, I was examined by a doctor who said "It is not possible!"

"Obviously it is. I'm here. I was standing behind Private Ruette, a large man who took the brunt of the explosion. It is his blood on my clothes."

Yet again, my greatest cover is the disinclination of people to believe the impossible, or what they are certain is impossible.

Quiet settled on the front for about three weeks. "Quiet"

meaning that danger was limited to artillery fire and snipers, but neither side "going over the top" to engage in direct hand-to-hand combat. After dark, small patrols would crawl out into no-man's land to repair the barbed wire damaged by artillery. These patrols only rarely exchanged fire because men on both sides would rarely venture beyond their barbed wire into the real killing ground that lay between.

Our battalion commander, Lieutenant-Colonel Fournier, was a strange mixture. Conscientious, he shared life in the trenches with his men and argued repeatedly with regimental and division headquarters for better food, wine, clothing, cigarettes and anything else to ease our lot. However, this conscientiousness extended to his other duties. He prided himself on being a man of action. "Fighting is why we are here, fighting to get the Boche out of France." Thus, early in April, 1915, having reports from scouts and aircraft that our section of the front was thinly defended, he secured permission for a sneak attack before dawn. Unusually, Fournier did not want the customary artillery barrage preceding the attack—"Why tell them we're coming?" The attack was a low-intensity operation, designed to gain and hold a section of the
German trench and, it was hoped, cause them to pull back for fear of having us behind them. To that end the division committed only a small reserve to follow us into the breech—optimism was never lacking.

The night of the attack, we went out to open our barbed wire. It was difficult enough to get through one barrier under fire. At 4 AM we started off—keeping as low and quiet as possible and in hope that after the lull, the German sentries were not as alert as usual. For a few minutes, which of course seemed much longer, we made good progress and some of our men were actually at work cutting the German wire and no enemy had been seen. Suddenly, just in front of the wire, there was an explosion. By the standards of the artillery it was a very small explosion but in the quiet and dark it seemed as loud as anything could be. A man had tripped a mine.

Almost instantly, flares went up and gunfire came from the parapets. A few concealed machine guns can hold off a much larger force. It was too open to try to get back to our trench so we had no option except a bayonet charge through the few openings in the wire. Despite large casualties, we did achieve the trench. I doubt that a third of the 180 men of my company got there. The rest of the battalion, or what was left of it, were, as nearly as I could tell, still engaged in front of the trench and we were alone with Germans in the trench on both sides of us. And the prospect of a counter-attack. The trench was not long and regular like a canal, but had a zig-zag pattern designed for just this eventuality and the Germans were able to enfilade us without our having an effective response. I shouted an order to retreat; specifically, "Get the Hell out of here!" We used our last grenades to block quick access to our section.

I was always able to leave last like a good commander, a practice that caused more questions than admiration. Just as I crawled out, a lone German with a flamethrower came running up and engulfed me in flames. Shaking off my burning uniform I tried to shoot him only to find that the flame had incapacitated my rifle. As I ran the few yards toward him with my bayonet, he did not move. He just stood fully composed. As I raised my bayonet, he dropped to his knees and said in a soft voice, "Bitte, lieb'Gott. Bitte." I drove the bayonet down into his chest just below the collar bone. He didn't make a sound as I pulled the blade out. He just looked at me, stoic and unblinking, even serene, for a couple of seconds, closed his eyes and fell forward.

That soldier continues to haunt me; ironic, a vampire being haunted. Was his "please, dear God" directed to me, thinking I was God? Was he begging to be spared or had he accepted his death and praying to be taken to heaven? Later, when the war seemed without end, soldiers would accept death as a release from the mud, fear, rats, and lice. But this was before such despair. His face as he knelt before me is one of very few I remember well.

Such thoughts were for later. Now I had to get back to my lines. Germans, realizing that this was not the beginning of a major attack, were beginning to emerge from the trench and shooting at me. I ran toward the French trench, no doubt puzzling the Germans on the sudden loss of their marksmanship. I stopped in a shell hole to take a uniform and rifle from one of our losses. The Germans did not pursue me across no-man's land.

Fournier had been wounded and his men had carried him back. Not all officers were beneficiaries of such solicitude. He was being treated behind the trench while waiting evacuation to a hospital. He asked why I was wearing a private's uniform. I told him I had been hit by a flamethrower but had managed to get out of my uniform before being burned. You will note how a small truth can be used to conceal a large lie.

"Everyone says that you have more lives than a cat." But he did not sound convinced.

That was the last time I saw Fournier. He recovered and returned to the front but I do not know if he survived the war. His type rarely do.

The new battalion commander transferred me to the rear, explaining that the "ignorant poilus," reversing themselves, were now afraid to be with me, that I attracted Death to others but not to myself.

Fortunately, shortly after this Italy entered the war on the side of the Allies and I asked to resign so that I could join my Italian unit. A more sensitive man would have been offended by the speed and eagerness with which my request was granted.

Having discovered that I was not fitted for modern warfare, I went to Barcelona. I felt out of place in this war. I had trained for real combat—man to man, armed only with what you could carry and knew how to use. Certainly, there had been artillery for a couple of centuries, but it only threw a heavy ball. If one was not directly in its path there was little danger. Now cannons threw hundreds of pounds of explosives killing everyone within several yards. In the Great War more men lost their lives to artillery than to rifles and machine guns. The randomness of artillery took a great psychological toll on soldiers; always on your mind was the knowledge that a shell could land any moment. One common fear was that of being buried alive in the collapse of the trench or dugout. I shared that fear; despite the passage of seven centuries the memory of my burial was undimmed. Machine guns were another descent into barbarism, spraying fire indiscriminately, no ability needed or satisfaction gained by pitting yourself against an equal whom you could see and who could see you. And it only gets worse. A continent away someone looking at a computer screen guides a mechanical assassin to "terminate" a target. It may be efficient but it is murder, not war.

3

Getting to Barcelona was not as easy as before the war. The French authorities were rigorously checking for deserters. As an Italian I wondered if the French, in a spirit of Allied cooperation, would deport me to Italy as I tried to cross the border. Most train stock had been diverted to the war effort and that, combined with the plea that I needed time to wrap up after three years in Paris, permitted me almost three weeks to find an alternate identity.

I did have a fairly wide choice. The war had brought many more foreigners to France: military volunteers, newsmen, relief organizations, and others. The task was to find a man whose description on his papers could reasonably be expected to fit me. I spent several days going to places where young men congregate, bars and bistros high on the list. It was not as easy as you might think. I have ordinary build and looks, not particularly memorable, which has often been to my advantage. The difficulty is in finding someone who is both somewhat untethered from society and has the identity I seek. An additional complication that the war brought was the rule that passports have a photograph so I had to find someone who looked enough like me in a bad photograph to pass any checkpoints. A little over a week of buying drinks and striking up conversations with dead ends —French or English soldiers were off limits because one would not be allowed to leave France, or men who seemed to be widely enough known whose disappearance would cause more publicity than I wanted—there was success. An American from Ohio who was free-lancing for local newspapers and had been in France less than a week. Hampered by very poor French, he was having trouble connecting. In my Italian-accented English, I explained my circumstance and offered to give him an interview on both life in the trenches and Italy's prospects in the war. He jumped at the chance and was so happy he actually paid for the drinks.

When I began my search I prepared a letter to a man with a common name—Joseph St. Jean—to leave on the body. No address of course, just a letter.

When I showed difficulty pronouncing and spelling his name he kindly took his passport from his jacket to help me. I had my new identity.

We took a walk along the Seine during which he had my story and at the end of which I had his papers. We found a fairly secluded spot between bushes. He carried a portfolio from which he withdrew a pad of paper and pencil. As I talked and paced, he sat cross-legged on the ground and wrote. It was getting on to six in the evening but May brought longer days and it was still light enough. As often occurs even in large cities, the came a moment when no one was within sight of us. Pacing behind and still talking, I took a cord from my pocket and slipped it around his neck, pulling it taut and jerking him backwards deeper into the bushes. He struggled for perhaps three minutes and then it was over. I dragged him a little further so we were not visible from the walk. I took his passport, wallet and a letter from his pockets and put my letter where he had had his. I was an American again. During the Civil War, I had been an Italian immigrant fighting for the Union and left in 1887 as an American.

With my Italian papers and a good word from the embassy, I was able to buy a ticket from Paris to Nice. At Lyons the train was commandeered to bring supplies to the front, a common occurrence. Several hours later I was on a very crowded train to Nice. There I became an American. After a couple of days I was able to get a train to Montpellier, from there to Perpignan and finally, eight days out from Nice, to Barcelona. On the French side of the border the exit guard looked at the passport and then back to me several times but in the end gave me the benefit of whatever doubt he had. On the Spanish side, the check was perfunctory. The neutral Spanish were not looking for deserters.

I remained in Barcelona for the remainder of the war. Once the United States got in I really had no place to go. I no more wanted to be an American soldier than I did for any other nationality.

Once in Barcelona I rented the customary two apartments, one under my then current American name in a middle-class neighborhood, which I kept as long as I was there, and a smaller one under an assumed name in a working-class area which I changed several times a year. The latter was, shall we say, my dining room. I did not like that arrangement but was not allowed to buy a house as I usually did. When I mentioned this to a Barcelonan acquaintance, he said that there was still a lot of bitterness against the United States for the Spanish-American War, then less than twenty year past.

4

Near the end of the war, with the hunger coming on, seeking prey of an evening, I saw a young man a little larger than I speaking French to a policemen who obviously did not understand a word. The young man was holding a small loaf of bread pleading "I'm hungry. I'll work for it." A third man, the shop owner, was looking at the young man repeating "Thief! He tries to steal my bread." The policeman was trying to take the bread, which was being cradled close to the young man's body. I intervened, explaining to the policemen, gave the shopkeeper a peseta for the bread, telling him to keep the change. The shopkeeper gave a small smile, shrugged his shoulders and said "I did not understand. Times are difficult. Certainly, I would have let him help for the loaf of bread." Before he could be put to the test, he disappeared back into the store. All the while, the young man was stuffing bread into his mouth as fast as he could swallow. I am not certain that he even bothered to chew.

I had long since learned that a hungry and lonely man was the easiest prey. A warm smile, some food and the offer of a job bought trust and gratitude; desperation overcame suspicion. The same is not true of a woman in a similar position who generally suspects base motives, but will almost always succumb to necessity.

I told him that I didn't have enough money to buy a meal (a lie) but that I had food for supper at my apartment (also a lie) and invited him to join me. He accepted—no surprise. By this time, he had consumed the whole loaf of bread and it was still early for supper so I offered wine and cheese to hold us.

The man's name was Denis and he was a deserter from the French Army. Wounded in 1916 and returned to the front upon recovery, he had been at Verdun during the mutiny of 1917 (though actually more a sit-down strike than mutiny, the soldiers maintained their positions but refused to attack). An important part of Petain's effort to restore morale was to rotate personnel regularly between the front line and the rear, as well as allowing more frequent leaves. Denis' home was in in the southwest, a farm a few kilometers from Foix. Given leave in March, 1918 he resolved to desert. He wept as he spoke of the friends and comrades lost over nearly four years of war—seeing them shot, ripped apart by machine guns or artillery, or simply vanishing. "I hear the screams of the dying every night." From the front, he took a train to Perpignan, from there to connect to Foix. On the train he befriended a soldier who was very ill with tuberculosis and had been discharged. Denis stole the man's discharge papers, left the train at the next stop and hiked into Spain. Feeling guilty, he said was sure that Guy, whose paper it was, would be granted another discharge if he lived long enough to ask.

Having put a sleeping draught in his wine, I listened with increasing impatience as he talked, becoming apprehensive that the sedative was too weak. Another glass of wine with a little more sedative. I did not want to kill him; it is much easier to feed while the heart is beating. Denis was in full nostalgia, speaking of his childhood. Finally he yawned. Shaking himself, he said "I don't understand why I feel tired, usually I can't even sleep through the night."

"A rough day?" I asked.

"No." He frowned and looked at his glass. "What have you given me?" He tried to jump up, but was slowed by the narcotic, giving me time to rise to meet his attack. Even so, he staggered me and we fell, knocking over a small lamp table. We wrestled a few seconds when I was able to grab a heavy glass ashtray that had fallen from the table and smash it into his head, just above the ear. He went still.

A rap on the door. "Jesus, now what!" I got up, went to the door and opened it just enough to see a man of about sixty. With one shoulder on the wall and the other propped against the edge of the door allowing an opening of about three inches, I was sure he could not see in.

"I heard noise from this apartment and I thought I should check that everything is all right."

"Everything is fine. Clumsy oaf that I am, I tripped on the rug and knocked over a table when I fell." He did not leave.

"Is there anything I can do? You look like you've been in a fight." He smiled.

"Yes. I'm afraid the table won. I'm..."

"You're going to have a black-and-blue mark on your fore-head."

"Oh. Thank you so much for your concern," (a lie so outrageous that I nearly gagged saying it) "I'd better put something on it." I closed the door. I checked my forehead, puzzled at what he saw. There was some blood that had to be Denis's from the fight.

Just in time. Denis let out a soft moan and moved a bit. The man was indestructible! Taking the straight razor from my pocket, I finally got my meal. Rarely have I have to work so hard for one. I put the razor in his hand, straightened out the room, cleaned myself up, waited until 10, and left unseen.

I read the newspapers every day. As anticipated, it took a while for the body to be discovered. I had given a month's rent and there were still about three weeks to run. In the warmth of April, it took less than the three weeks for the odor to excite investigation. At first, identified with Guy's papers, the police concluded he had committed suicide because of the tuberculosis but were "puzzled" by his using another name to rent the apartment. The article included a bit saying that a neighbor had talked to the man and found him "disheveled and disoriented." The bloating of the body concealed that Denis was a robust young man, not at all tubercular. Within a week, the French had revealed the substitution of the papers and that he was in fact a deserter. The new, final conclusion was suicide from shame and remorse, the false name used to further conceal his real identity.

5

The Great War, which includes what is known as the Second World War, destroyed my Europe, the Europe I was born into, the Europe that had existed, with few breaks, since the Roman Empire. There was a confidence, a pride often spilling into arrogance that Europeans were the center of the world. When fortified by Christianity we set out to guide humanity through this world and prepare it for the next. All things were possible and the idea of progress, that tomorrow will be better than today and the day after even better, was accepted as absolute truth. Between the sixteenth and nineteenth centuries this attitude allowed us to steal two-thirds of the earth from its rightful owners and remake it largely in our own image.

The irony is that the class that had built this Europe, the aristocrats with their sense of *noblesse oblige*, are the ones who failed their greatest test. They were closely bound by blood, interests, and education, hunted together, raced their yachts against each other, took their "cures" together at the fashionable spas and had more in common with each other than with the people of their own countries. No one wanted the war, but they did not want other things more strongly: Loss of prestige or losing an ally by not backing it fully. Thus, Germany and France were pulled along by their more irresponsible allies, Austria-Hungary and Russia. They all saw the abyss but went resolutely to the edge believing that someone else would stop before they all fell over. But then, in Sir Edward Grey's apt metaphor, the lights went out.

SS

Looking for hunting ground in 1931, my attention was naturally drawn to Germany where the Nazis and Communists were beating and killing each other on the streets. A perfect environment—bodies were not only found almost every morning, they were expected. This time I felt I needed a German identity because I was getting involved in politics; I did not care which party. Munich was the center of the violence so I went to the other end of Germany, Silesia, and after three weeks' search found a young farm boy who had just arrived in Breslau with all his papers. Then on to Munich in my new persona as a brutal young thug.

My first night in Munich, at a beer garden I sat next to a uniformed young man keeping time with the oompah-pah band by softly banging his seidel on the table. I introduced myself and inquired about his uniform. His name was Volker Schmidt. He said with great pride that he belonged to the *Schutzstaffel*, "Protection Squad," mostly known by its initials, SS.

"What do you protect?"

"Germany!"

"From what?"

"Her enemies: Communists, Jews, Gypsies, queers—all the degenerate vermin."

He said this quite light-heartedly, as if it were the most obvious thing in the world. Maybe it was, I have heard the same or similar in many countries at many times. Mostly it was just talk.

He went on, "Actually we began as just protection for the Führer, Adolf Hitler, and other leaders of the party but recently Reichsführer-SS Himmler has turned us into a strike force." He looked me up and down, nodded and said, "We can always use good men."

"I need a job. I'm good with my fists and with guns. I have hunted since I was seven or eight."

Over the next couple of hours he filled me in on the workings and principles of the SS. On leaving we agreed to meet the next morning when he would bring me to his station and introduce me to his officers.

Nothing to it. Thanks to Volker I was able to say all the right wrong things and was welcomed. I thought that these amateurs were in for a surprise, that while they were playing tough soldier, real disappearances would be occurring. I was soon to learn that these men were deadly serious. The rest of the world took a little more time.

Nineteen thirty-two was an election year in Germany which kept us busy intimidating Hitler's opponents. Eighty-five year old Paul von Hindenburg, running reluctantly because his backers convinced him that only he could defeat Hitler, was elected on the second ballot. The political stalemate continued and in January, 1933 Hindenburg grudgingly named Hitler Chancellor, surrounded by a cabinet of politicians who would keep him in check. In any political contest I can remember, reasonable men who abide by the rules invariably lose to the ruthless men who will do anything to gain power. Thus it was.

During the campaign, Hitler came to Munich and I was part of the Honor Guard at the rally. Hitler was a strange phenomenon. He was mesmerizing as an orator, with complete command of his voice and body, though with the gift of making it all appear emotionally spontaneous. He held the audience rapt. They cheered, screamed, swooned, wept. Later, one could not remember what he said. There was no content, just emotion and vitriol. Reading the speeches in the quiet of one's room, they were vacuous platitudes interspersed with diatribes against enemies who were destroying Germany. When, however, Hitler was in front of an audience screaming that Germany was being destroyed and he would save it, he would end the humiliation of Versailles and restore Germany to her destiny, his charisma made it easy to believe, and desperate people wanted to believe.

Despite that, despite the almost 25% unemployment, despite the depression, both economic and psychic, the Germans rejected Hitler and Ernst Thälmann, the Communist candidate, staying with the safe, stolid Hindenburg.

Between joining the SS in November, 1931 and June 30, 1934, I managed to feed regularly, protected by my uniform. Seeing the uniform caused the men I told to come along to come along. When I got them to my dining room they were dead before they realized where they were. The bodies were buried in the cellar. If there were an inquiry into a disappearance, the information that he went with the SS ended the investigation. I managed to pretend to perform my official duties without, or rarely, hurting anyone. I know you wonder if this is just an excuse. Nothing I can do about that.

In late spring, 1934 there was the most serious domestic crisis that Hitler had to face. Hindenburg and the army were concerned that the 3,000,000 man para-military Storm Troopers (SA) under Ernst Röhm were a threat to the state and that it was planning on absorbing the regular army. They told Hitler to disband them or face dismissal. The army was the one power in Germany which could make good that threat; Hitler listened.

The SA represented the left wing of the Nazis, like Röhm and the Strasser brothers, who took the "Socialist" in the party's name seriously. The right-wing Nazis— Göring, Himmler, Goebbels—were filling Hitler with rumors of a coup by the SA. The SS, under Himmler and his deputy, Heydrich, were ordered to liquidate the SA leadership. I was a member of a squad given a subsidiary raid on a large house in the Munich suburbs that was used by SA officers for sex and games with their catamites. Though the Nazi leadership had long known of the homosexuality in the SA and done nothing, it was now used to blacken their reputations.

I was picked up by Volker with a cheerful "We're off to kill some homos." There were six of us. Someone asked if we were enough, the SA had weapons.

Our team leader, Erich, gave us the layout. "There are six rooms occupied. The landlady is our spy and she called saying everyone has gone to their rooms with brandy and beer. Anyway they're all in bed with their cocks up each other's arses. No problems. Just go in shooting."

Volker was quivering with anticipation. "We're cleaning out the scum."

I have never known anyone so excited and happy at the prospect of killing.

I went because the hunger was coming on and I was plotting a strategy to use one of the murders for dinner.

We stopped on the street, a little way from the house and walked silently. We had soft soled shoes, were not in uniform but wearing black jerseys and trousers. We had stripped anything that might make noise from our clothes. We carried our pistols in our waist bands. We were let in by our mole, the only woman in the house, who was "disgusted by the shameless sins committed here."

There were four bedrooms on the first and two on the second storeys—European style, ground floor, then first, second, etc.

I was one of the four assigned the first storey, Volker and another man went up. When they reached the top of the stairs, on a signal from Erich we all moved.

Three of the doors were partially closed. I tried the knob of my room. The door was not locked. There were two in bed, naked. A man of about 35 who was on top of a boy and on my entry rolled over on his back, reaching for a pistol on the table next to the bed. I fired twice. One hit him in the stomach below the ribcage, the other on the right side of his chest. He rolled off the bed, leaving two blood stained holes in the mattress, and fell face down. For a few seconds he tried to get up. Raising his hips a couple of inches and put his hands as if to push up, coughed up a little blood, but the hips fell and he did not move again. The boy looked no more than 16 and, oddly enough, was very much the Teutonic ideal, blond and blue-eyed, slim and handsome.

The boy was sobbing, face streaked with tears. "Please... please, don't shoot...please...I'm nothing...please...don't kill me...I'm just a toy...please don't shoot...please." He was trembling, his voice shaking.

I closed the door, turned the key and put the pistol back in my waistband,

"May I play with the toy?" I smiled.

He gasped, it may have been the first breath he took since I barged in.

"Oh, yes... yes...thank you. Please...yes...thank you." His voice still quavered.

As I moved toward him, he reached out both arms to embrace me. I did the same, with a razor concealed in my right hand. A quick slash and my mouth was on the wound. I am not often given to remorse and this boy was not an exception. He was dead anyway, the squad would have seen to it. Also, for you sentimentalists, he thought he had been saved and died without knowing differently.

Normally after feeding I like a period of peace and quiet. But I had to clean up and get out of the room before anyone discovered the door was locked.

I went into the hall and heard two shots followed by an almost continual screams of pain, broken only to get air enough to scream again. I ran upstairs toward the sound and found Volker in a room standing astride an SS face down with two exit wounds in his back, a naked man dead on the floor, another on the bed and the screaming man sitting on his heels on the floor, also naked, holding his genitals, with blood streaming down his thighs and onto the floor. Above his hands was a visible bullet hole in the middle of his abdomen. Volker was laughing.

"The son of a bitch killed Horst. He tried to shoot me but I got him right in the balls. Listen to him! Did you ever hear anything like that?"

One of the others yelled from the hall, "Let's get out of here."

The man on the floor stopped screaming to say, "Kill me. Please kill me."

Volker shrugged and spread his arms. He smiled, "No rush." He fired his pistol into the left knee, and the man resumed screaming.

That was the moment I decided to kill him.

"What's that racket?" Erich was at the doorway.

Volker told him, "He killed Horst and I'm making him pay."

"We don't have time for that shit." Erich shouted and fired his piston into the top of the man's head, causing the skull to explode, brain, blood, and bone scattering. His torso rocked a little back then slumped forward, what was left of his head resting on his knees.

Volker almost jumped with joy, "Beautiful, so beautiful!"

It took a few weeks to find a location and a method of getting him there. Then it was devising a way to get him to come with me without anyone knowing he was coming with me.

Just as I was ready, history intervened. On August 2, President von Hindenburg died. There followed two weeks of memorials and parades. Hitler declared that the presidency was so associated with Hindenburg that there was no possible successor; he would remain chancellor and assume the simple title of "Leader."

I remade my arrangements and one Monday evening, when he had told me he would be home alone to study for a promotional examination, I drove to his apartment.

"Grab your books and a bathing suit, I've got a cabin on Würmsee for three days. We can get some sun and swimming as well as cramming. I arranged a couple days' leave for us." He was ready in minutes. We were in our uniforms. They gave us privileges.

Lake Würm, now Lake Starnberg, is only a short drive from Munich. I had, naturally, taken the cabin under another name and address with papers taken off of one of my prey. We arrived, I unlocked the door and allowed Volker to proceed ahead of me. I slipped a garrote over his head and pulled it tight. I used a flexible wire with reverse teeth that held the loop and could not be loosened. He whirled around, drew his pistol and fired.

"Now look what you've done to my uniform." I said it as if I were speaking to a misbehaving child. He fired three times more before I knocked it out of his hand. He clawed at the wire, badly scratching his neck. His eyes were almost popping out of his head, from fear or strangulation or both. He was making sorts of choking, gurgling sounds. I drew close and he grabbed my neck in an attempt to choke me.

"I'm here to take you to Hell." I put my mouth close to his ear, "You are going to Hell and all the tortures of Hell for ever and ever and ever." He was shaking his head and his mouth was moving but the sounds were getting weaker. I chanted "Hell, hell, we're going to hell," until he fell, gave one last convulsive spasm and was still. The whole episode lasted perhaps four minutes. I hoped I succeeded in convincing him that I was indeed a minion of Satan and that he knew terror at inexorable, eternal torture. I believe it is the only sadistic act I ever committed. No one was more deserving.

I drove back to Munich. The next morning we all wondered why the ever punctual Volker had not come in. Telephone calls were unanswered and in the afternoon two men went to his apartment. The landlord let them in and everything looked perfectly normal. On Saturday, the rental ended and the body was found. The investigation revealed that the renter had himself disappeared three month before. Though blamed on vague "enemies of the state," the murder remained unsolved. His friends did wonder how an excellent shot like Volker could fire four times and hit nothing but the wall. The lack of blood on the floor seemed to indicate complete misses. I participated in his elaborate SS march and funeral, setting a personal standard for hypocrisy I have yet to match.

I left Germany within a few months. Taking leave, I acquired a new identity in Vienna and betook myself to Buenos Aires.

ONE LAST DUTY

1

I arrived in Buenos Aires in March, 1935, in the middle of what the Argentines call the "Infamous Decade" following the military coup of 1930. While the Great Depression was severe and there was much workplace turmoil and many strikes, life for a well-off Viennese expatriate was more than comfortable. Culture, especially music, was equal to Europe or North America—I even learned to tango. I travelled throughout the country and fell in love with the Andes and the glaciers. They were beyond anything I had ever seen. The Alps and Rockies are spectacular, but still inferior to the Andes.

By this time I had learned to bluff my way through the occasionally inevitable meal. I would take a bite, look puzzled and say something to the effect, "Excellent, very interesting flavor." This would trigger a discussion around the table of the dish's merits compared to other restaurants or at home. Within a year I had a good basic knowledge of the more popular dishes and was able to sound as if I really knew what I was talking about.

The Depression had driven thousands of impoverished rural residents into the city whose anonymous, rootless lives made hunting as easy as I have ever known.

Buenos Aires, however, is seared into my memory because of

a foggy, rainy day in August, 1939. I was driving on Santa Fe Avenue in my 1937 Hillman Minx when a car came through the intersection at Azcuénaga because its brakes failed to catch—a common hazard in the days of drum brakes on wet streets—and crashed into the driver's side of my car. I slid into the next lane and collided with a car which was pushed into the oncoming lane and was hit in its turn. Brakes squealed, tires skidded, and horns blared above the sound of multiple collisions. At the end, vehicles were tangled in a mass. I was trapped, pinned into my seat barely able to wiggle, much less get out. A crowd gathered, police and emergency crews arrived. I was close enough to the outside of the jumble for people to gawk and wonder aloud how long I would live. Even worse, two or three had cameras and were taking pictures. As I was not the only one trapped I did not have everyone's attention. This was long before the "jaws of life" were developed and it took almost two hours for a couple of welders to cut me loose. Others took even longer; it seemed that the police had been able to gather almost every welder in the city. Then came the argument about going to the hospital amid the chatter of the crowd wondering audibly at how I could be alive, much less able to walk away. A couple of the more pious fell to their knees proclaiming a miracle. I assured the medics that I had no pain and was quite resilient, moreover there were others who needed their attention much more. Even with centuries of practice I could not invent an explanation for having neither heartbeat nor pulse.

I was now famous, at least in Buenos Aires, the condition I fear most. The next day, I learned from the newspapers that fourteen cars were involved, five people were killed, and eleven were in the hospital, some in critical condition. Among the pictures of those involved were two of me; one, with my name, trapped in the car, the other of me standing and talking with a policeman with the caption "Incredible, he walked away."

I hid in my apartment for three days hoping the whole thing

would be quickly forgotten. On the fourth day I ventured out and within the first block someone pointed to me and another actually came up to me and asked how I managed to get out alive. I went back and packed. The next morning I went to the airport and got on the first plane I could, a flight to Havana. I did not have time to pave the dining room cellar. More truthfully, I completely forgot about it in my haste.

I stayed in Havana three days and then flew to Tampa.

2

Several days after arriving in Tampa, Germany invaded Poland and World War II began. When Germany annexed Austria in 1938, I had to turn in my Austrian passport for a German one. I was certain that the United States would eventually get into the war and I did not want to become an enemy alien. Getting a new identity thus became critical. Having left Buenos Aires so precipitously, I did not have time to make the usual financial transactions, just a letter of credit from my Argentine bank, which was owned by a British bank which I feared might impound my funds at any moment. I needed to open an American account under my new identity so I could access the bulk of my money then held in a Swiss trust.

Instead of assuming someone else's identity, I thought to manufacture an entirely new person. Early in September I visited several Synagogues and asked to speak to the Rabbi. I explained that I was a Jew from Austria in the United States illegally and was afraid of being caught and deported back to the Nazis, pointing out that the country had turned back a ship of refugees and I did not want to expose myself by asking for asylum. Could he connect me to someone who could get me a birth certificate and other papers? Also, I had the means to pay "expenses." All were sympathetic and all but one did not know what they could do. The one, Rabbi Shulman said he had an idea and would contact people and hoped to have something for me in a day or two. I gave him my address at a cheap hotel near the docks.

Two days later he called and asked me to come to his office that evening, he thought he had a solution. When I arrived a woman of about fifty, Elaine, was there. Upon being introduced, she nodded twice and said, "I will tell you something that I have only told Rabbi Shulman. My son was born in 1916, in Brooklyn, and died in the flu epidemic in 1918, which also took my husband. I left New York and over the next several years worked my way down the east coast. I'm good with numbers and became a bookkeeper in Philadelphia, Washington and Atlanta before coming to Tampa eight years ago. The point of this is that I still have my son's birth certificate, notarized and everything. The Rabbi explained your situation and thinks you could use Sebastian's identity."

At times I can almost believe that something is watching over me. This seemed too lucky to be a coincidence. Then I realize that there is no reason why anything would wish me to continue my existence as the world's most prolific serial killer.

I expressed my sympathy for her loss and thanked her saying "This is so much better than having a forged birth certificate." Because her friends knew her as a childless widow, a son could not suddenly show up. For the third time in little more than a month I would be moving on. I took the train to New Orleans where I established a residence and finally got my finances in order. With that I found a dean of a small college who, for a fee, would give me a diploma, Class of 1938 and a transcript on file to use as reference. I suppressed my vanity and accepted a B average since anything much better would cause people to wonder why they did not remember me, just in case there were inquiries.

3

One year later, the Selective Training and Service Act of 1940 became law. It required all men between 21 and 36 to register.

The Act was a bureaucratic masterpiece with dozens of categories, local draft boards and a national lottery. I pondered finding a new identity and leaving the country, but there was really nowhere I wanted to go. Everyplace I felt at home was either occupied, at war or recovering from a war. As I said earlier, war was no longer an adventurous test of skill; it had become a deadly game of chance. I registered along with several acquaintances.

My number did not come up until January, 1942 when Selective Service greatly raised the number of draftees in the aftermath of Pearl Harbor. The induction center gave us tests and interviews and a medical appointment for the next day. Knowing what was coming I had made my plans. Telling an acquaintance, whose number had not yet been drawn but was about to volunteer, that I was slightly asthmatic, and while in no way incapacitated, I was still fearful of being rejected. In that patriotic time, he was completely sympathetic. I provided him with my papers to take the examination in my place, which he passed. With my new medical certification I was off to war again.

4

Toward the end of the Second World War. I was an American soldier and had landed a few days after D-Day. I was assigned liaison to the French forces who more moving southeast from Paris while the Americans and British moved to the east and north. On April 25, 1945 we crossed from France into Germany, not far from the Swiss border. The fighting had largely subsided, with small pockets of Germans who were generally ready to surrender. That night, while the unit I was with got some much needed sleep, I took advantage of a bright moon and went hunting. I had gone about two miles when I saw car lights and heard engines not far away that seemed to be coming in my direction. Moving cautiously toward the sound, a break in the trees showed a road and two German Staff cars were almost opposite me. I took cover and when they had passed, I went on the road and saw a house a few hundred yards beyond with a single window illuminated on the ground floor. Following aside the road from the trees, I could see or hear no activity. Sneaking up to the window with the light I looked in and saw only one occupant, an old man sitting in an armchair, awake, head back, staring at the ceiling. He was wearing a dark, double-breasted suit that fit loosely, as if the man it covered had shrunk. It was Pétain. The front door was unlocked, the room to my left.

"Monsieur le Maréchal?"

"Yes. Who are you?"

I snapped to attention, saluted and announced, "Captain Smith, United States Army, sir."

"So the Americans will take me," softly, almost a sigh.

"No, sir. I am attached to a French regiment and they will be here in the morning."

He nodded, "Good. That is as it should be."

"You seem to be here alone, sir. How is that?"

"The Germans were bringing me to Switzerland with false papers, but I refused. I told them I would tell the border guards who I am and that I wanted to go to France. They found this house and drove off. Now I wait."

"Why?"

"I have one last duty."

He began to talk. Though I would say something from time to time, to encourage him when he faltered or to ask a question, I present his words without interruption as I remember them, if not verbatim, certainly in essence.

"Everything I have done, I have done for France, my idea of France. You know, I joined the Army in 1876. Imagine, almost seventy years. At that time, France was deep in humiliation. We had lost the war with Germany, which we ought to have won, lost Alsace-Lorraine.

"Of course, the generals learned all the wrong lessons. They trained the army to charge, always advance, courage, *élan*, character will triumph over gunfire. Insane. I argued against it, let the enemy attack our firepower and when they have suffered the casualties, we counter-attack their reduced and dispirited troops. My career suffered. I was promoted more slowly than my contemporaries.

"When war came in 1914, the generals charged across the frontier to recapture Alsace-Lorraine and in ten days had a few hectares and 150,000 casualties. The only lesson was 'more,' more soldiers, more artillery, more firepower which only led to more casualties. The only surprise about the mutiny was that it was three years coming. The mutiny was not against France or the war, it was against stupidity and slaughter. With the Armistice the slaughter ended but the stupidity continued. The peace treaty guaranteed another war—too harsh to conciliate Germany, too lenient to prevent her becoming powerful again. Foch was right, dismember Germany into its old countries, France overseeing the Rhineland.

"Unlike 1940, the poilus fought. They went to war well-trained and well-armed. They suffered terribly but they fought on because they believed. I do not know what happened after the war. The war took our best, almost a million-and-a-half killed, over four million wounded, the heart of the nation, men between 18 and 50 and also took the heart out of those who survived. The politicians said that the treaty, the League of Nations, would protect us; that a strong army was against the spirit of Locarno. Even after 1933 with Hitler building weapons as fast as he could, the politicians did nothing. That was the year Weygand advised the government that the French Army was no longer a serious fighting force. The government, under

Daladier, took this advice as an opportunity to reduce the army further and decrease pay.

"In 1935 I wrote that the army needed better training, a better reserve system, air power, and armor. The country talked about me and then elected the Popular Front. They chose a little extra jam on their bread rather than security. The French are not worthy of France.

"Not satisfied with that, in 1938, they betrayed our only worthwhile ally and threw away the 40 excellently trained and equipped divisions of Czechoslovakia. Madness! It was madness. Then, at the moment of maximum weakness, they go to war in defense of the indefensible—Poland, which had grabbed its piece in the dismemberment of Czechoslovakia. Indefensible because the Hitler-Stalin treaty meant that Poland would face a two-front war when they could not defend one. They were useless to us. The idiots thought they were safe behind the Maginot Line.

"The Maginot Line was an excellent conception to give us a defensive line that could be held by relatively few soldiers. Allowing us to concentrate most of our Army against the numerically superior Germans to even the disparity. But, and it is a large but, the strategy envisioned strong air and armored forces protected by the Maginot to thrust in behind the German front as it came through Belgium. Where were the planes? Where were the tanks? Too expensive! We cannot waste the people's money on such things!

"And when the catastrophe they have made inevitable falls, the politicians come running to Pétain like children who have gotten into trouble running to their Papa, 'Save us! Save us!' But it is too late. The army has dissolved, the people beg for peace. I am called a defeatist. Is it defeatism to stop a slaughter? The politicians ensured that the Army was able to do nothing but die. I prevented that and the people of France applauded. The last time I was in Paris, two months before the invasion of Normandy, tens of thousands came out to cheer me. Today, those same thousands will come out and cheer as I am hanged. That is why I return to France. I have one last duty.

"When France was occupied, millions collaborated and continued to collaborate until the Germans retreated. No country can live with that sin so I return to expiate their sin. Now they will say 'It was that wicked old man. He betrayed us.' Then they can go on, comforting themselves that they were true patriots led astray. I will take upon myself all the guilt of France so she may have a new beginning."

He said all of this softly, matter-of-factly, without any sense of nobility or martyrdom, just reciting the Orders of the Day.

I spoke, "Will they really hang you?"

"What does it matter? I am nearly 90." He raised his hand and moved it back and forth as if he were brushing something away. "Pétains come and go. France is eternal."

Dawn was breaking, I heard vehicles approaching.

"The French are here, Monsieur le Maréchal. I must leave now." I saluted.

He nodded and I went out the back door as he rose to go to the front.

Charles de Gaulle wrote that Petain's decision to return to France was courageous.

BELLA ITALIA

1

A couple of years after the Second World War I moved to Rome, still home after all these centuries. I wanted to see how the old city had come through the war. It had been only forty-five years since I had left Naples but I thought the chance of my being recognized in Rome was negligible enough to risk. And for the first time since I was Octavian, I lived as an Italian in Italy. I invented a name and chose as a birthplace a town in Calabria that had been destroyed in the war. The authorities were understanding, accepting that all proofs of my identity had disappeared into the wreckage of war, and provided me with new papers.

Happily, Rome had been declared an open city and largely escaped the war without damage. Occasionally, rarely, humans are capable of rational behavior and they saved what remains of their beginnings in Europe. When I arrived early in 1947, before the Marshall Plan, the Italian economy was moribund and unemployment high. There was one brilliant exception to the stagnation. Out of this unpromising soil, in the three years after the war, with minuscule budgets and largely non-professional actors, grew films—*The Bicycle Thief, Open City, Paisan*—that re-created Italian cinema, made movies art, and have inspired filmmakers ever since.

I took a small apartment on Via Principe Amadeo, between the main railroad station and Santa Maria Maggiore and bought a new Fiat Topolino ("little mouse" but also the Italian name for Mickey Mouse), a very small two seat coupe that began to put Italians back on the road after the war. Cute but not very comfortable. I used it for exploring the area between Rome and the Amalfi peninsula, Pompeii, and Paestum, generally avoiding Naples. Also for hunting. Gas rationing limited driving just for pleasure. Unlike everyone else, I needed gas more than food, at any rate the food that was available with the coupons, so I could trade coupons, food for gas.

After getting as much mileage out of the Topolino as possible, I purchased a larger 1952 Fiat 1900 sedan which increased my range and I put on thousands of kilometers driving around Italy, with occasional side trips to France, by the time I had to leave Rome in 1958. That car played its part in one of my more memorable hunting trips. As always the passenger seat had a waterproof cover in case I fed in the car. Toward the end of August, 1953, I drove out of Rome just wandering, looking for prey as the hunger was beginning. A hitchhiker was always vulnerable because it was often difficult for the police to determine where one had disappeared if, indeed, one was reported missing. I was driving roughly northeast from Rome, with no particular destination in mind on a lightly traveled road, Italy not yet prosperous enough to purchase the millions of cars that now clog the streets and highways. About sixty kilometers from Rome I saw a target. A man in his late teens or early twenties with a backpack, looking like what he turned out to be, a university student.

I rolled to a stop and called through the open window, "Where to?"

"Perugia. I'm at the University."

Excellent. The route would take us over the Apennines

where I was certain to find a deserted stretch of road for a private dinner. "Get in, I can pass through Perugia on my way to Bologna."

In reply to my comment that he could have chosen a busier road, Luca, as he introduced himself, said that he started here. He had spent the summer tutoring the son of a wealthy family at their summer villa. My asking how it went was evidently sympathetic enough to allow him to release the pent up frustrations.

"It was the worst twelve weeks of my life! Bad enough to make me a Communist! The boy, who is 14 thought of nothing but football and tennis, it was a constant struggle to get him to focus on his studies. No wonder his school was going to hold him back. I had to prepare him to take examinations so that he could be passed into the next class. Only the threat to tell his father got him to do anything. The mother treated me like one of the servants, with whom I had to eat, and watched constantly as if I would steal anything that wasn't nailed down, which did not keep her from bragging how expensive everything in the villa was."

He went on in this vein for a while then, having exhausted the subject, we went on to other topics: His plans for a career, my (made-up) partisan stories. Like many men who had never been to war, Luca thought it much more glamorous than it is.

"I wish I had been old enough to fight and kill some Germans, but I was only twelve when the war ended."

"There was a terrible price for killing Germans. Thousands of civilians were executed in reprisal."

"But isn't freedom worth it?"

"We thought so, but if we did nothing, the Allies would have won anyway and saved all those lives. Looking back, I have learned that the Communist and non-Communist partisans were really fighting to establish themselves to take over Italy after the war."

Meanwhile it had begun to rain, we had started to climb and were almost alone on the road. Then we heard a horn, first faintly but getting closer and louder. Suddenly around the curve ahead, a large truck, obviously out of control, came speeding toward us in the middle of the road. Instinctively, I jerked the car to the right and over we went. The right side of the road was at the edge of a gentle slope with no guard rail. When the car got to the mud, it gave way and we flipped over twice, from wheels to roof to wheels to roof to wheels and came to a stop. Without seat belts, we were tossed around but not as much as I would have thought. Before I could say anything, Luca shouted happily, "Wow! Can we do that again?"

I brought him to Perugia.

2

Tough car. No windows broken and except for a shallow dent in the roof, no damage. Very impressive for Fiat's new unit body construction even if the bounce was softened by the thick grass. The car started and in a few hundred meters the slope ended and I was able to get back on the road.

For those of you worried that I went hungry that night, relax. After dropping off Luca, I was walking around Perugia when a women, neither young nor pretty, asked me for money to buy a train ticket so she could get out of town. I always dress to look prosperous.

"Where are you going?"

"Anyplace the next train goes. I have to get out of here before my husband finds me." I noticed bruises on her arms and knew there were probably more covered by her dress.

"I am driving to Rome, would you like to join me?"

She appraised me for a few seconds, sighed and said "Oh, what the Hell. It can't get worse."

On that enthusiastic note she got into the car. I asked if she were hungry. Yes, so we stopped at a small grocer and I bought bread, cheese, and wine and walked to the car. I wondered when she had last eaten because she had gone through most of the bread and cheese and all of the wine within twenty kilometers. While eating she unburdened herself, inhibition lessened by the wine.

"I don't know what I'll do in Rome or anyplace for that matter. Look at me, I'm 36 and look 50. Back to factory, I guess. That's where I started and got married to get out. Sixteen years ago but it feels like sixty. He was a soldier and was always rough but he was at the front during the war so I didn't have to put up with him. When the war ended he got worse. He couldn't find a job except as a janitor at the school. He took it out on me. Worse, he thought our son wasn't his. He had been born after one of his leaves, but he refused to believe it. Four years ago he told the boy to get the out of his house. Seven years old! Can you believe? And just to look at them you know they are father and son. I threatened to go to the police and he beat me and said that he would kill me. The boy is with my sister, a war widow. I'll never see him again because that's where my husband will be looking for me. If I could make enough money, maybe I could..." she trailed off and began to cry softly.

Then, to my relief, she fell asleep; I do not like to fight with my prey, particularly women. By this time, the hunger and pain were overwhelming. I pulled into a dirt road screened from the main road by trees. When we stopped she stirred a little but did not have time to open her eyes. Back on the main road, in a few kilometers I found a turn off to a lake. I could not have planned it better. It was now getting dark but I was able to make out an escarp and, hoping that it ended in deep water, wrapped her in a blanket, tied weights around the body (I travel prepared) and rolled her over the edge. I checked her purse and found a name, Regina Binni, but no address. I marveled again at the names parents inflict, "Queen" for this poor woman, or naming me after an Emperor.

I cleaned up both myself and the car, then...?

3

I wondered if anyone in Perugia would remember Regina Binni talking to me and getting into the car. I wanted to settle with her husband but did not want to have someone associate me with the woman. Men who beat women and children are the poorest excuse for a man, in fact I do not consider them men at all. You may be screaming "Hypocrite!" at me, but I am a predator and whatever God or Satan expects of me, if anything, I still recognize that I can sometimes put my thumb on the scales of justice to right the balance. I went back to Perugia.

It was after nine when I arrived so I booked a hotel room. The next morning, after buying a newspaper in the unlikely event that it mentioned a disappearance, I walked around the city and realized that I did not really know what I was doing, not as rare a feeling as I should like. What was I hoping to find? I did not know whether she had lived in Perugia or had started her flight from another city. I was in a city of perhaps 120,000 people plus thousands of students at the university. The entire sequence of if her husband were in Perugia and if he reported her disappearance and if the newspaper carried the story and if his name and address were published meant that I was entirely dependent upon so many "ifs" that I had no control of my own. Not a comfortable feeling when one is planning a murder. In spite of that, I decided to give it a week.

After five days I was ready to give up. Perugia is an attractive small city, accent on "small," and wandering around the city was circumscribed by the possibility of meeting Luca. I was not certain I could explain why I chose to stay in Perugia rather than going on to the much larger and more exciting Bologna. On the sixth morning, however, there was a small item in the newspaper that eleven year old Michele Binni had made a missing person report on his mother, wife of Alessandro Binni. No address was given. The evening newspaper, however, had a picture of Mr. and Mrs. Binni, a separate one of Michele, and a request to come to the police with any information. Even better, it had the Binni address. Having spent some of the time cooped up in my hotel room studying a map of Perugia, I had become familiar with the city. It was dusk and I walked to his neighborhood, found the building and confirmed the name on the postbox, one of six, two to a floor. Outside, arbitrarily assigning odd numbers to the left and even to the right, I concluded that there were no lights on in his apartment. I settled in to wait. About an hour later, toward quarter of eight, Binni came home. As he went into the entrance, I ran in behind him.

"Signore Binni."

"What do you want?"

"I have a message from your wife."

A heavy, petulant sigh, "I don't care what the whore has to say. She can't come back."

That was the point at which if I had had any qualms they would have evaporated.

I drove a butcher knife into his solar plexus, his mouth opened to scream but I shoved a balled up handkerchief into it and pushed the knife further with all my weight behind it. I was almost leaning on him, forcing him to the wall. He put his hands on my shoulders to push me away but his strength was already fading. He began to slide down the wall. I pulled the knife out and stepped back. He slumped to the floor, sitting but listing to the right. I left.

The murder made the front page in the morning papers. The police were looking for Regina Binni. About noon I told the hotel manager I would be checking out the next morning.

"I hope you enjoyed your stay in Perugia."

"Not what I expected, but interesting."

The next day, on my way back to Rome, I buried the knife in the mountains. If Regina Binni's body was ever found, the Rome newspapers did not mention it

.

4

Nineteen fifty-eight and time to move on. After the usual search, I found a replacement identity. Walking home alone after an evening with acquaintances and the opera I was approached by a smiling young man who offered to give me great pleasure for 20,000 lire, which, as I recall, was about fifteen dollars.

"I am certain you could but I just left a woman who did."

"I can bring you again. Have you ever done it with a man?"

"Not yet but not now. I have had a long day and want to go home."

The smile was gone and he looked as if he was about to cry. "I'm hungry. I only do this to eat." It was a little after midnight and we were alone. I wondered how desperate he was. However, he made no move when I took out my wallet

"Here's for something to eat," I handed him a 10,000 lire note and a card with my dining room address, "If you would like a job, as a messenger, come tomorrow afternoon at two. That will give you the morning to get your identity papers and birth certificate that we need for the government's forms. The job includes a scooter if you have a license, otherwise a bicycle." A little extra temptation.

He came, of course. I knew that if he did not want the job he would want to go off with the scooter or bicycle. He had his papers and I gave him a cold panino which put him to sleep shortly after eating it.

In the several weeks that I remained in Rome getting a passport in my new name and generally finishing the usual chores, the newspapers had no story about the missing man. I wondered if he was that alone or was considered not important enough to mention.

THE PAST IS NEVER PAST

The telephone rang.

"Sebastian here."

"Sebastian? It's Michael. Can you I drop in? There's something you must see. I can't believe it and neither will you."

"There is much that I cannot believe but it happens anyway. I am free all afternoon, I can come at your convenience."

"Thanks. See you in about an hour."

London at the beginning of the Swinging Sixties. I had taken a flat in Barkston Gardens not far from the Earl's Court tube station and a small bungalow in a working class neighborhood for my dining room.

Soon after my arrival, I took a nursing course only to learn how to draw blood. Upon getting my certificate, I volunteered at a blood bank and became quite good at going into the vein instead of through it. As inventory control was very lax, I was able to lift the needles and plastic bags, one at a time and acquired a good supply, which I replenish by the same method or purchase from underpaid aides. I do not miss cutting an artery and having to clean up after. Blood will keep 24 hours in a refrigerator so I do not have to gorge myself. Half today, half tomorrow, much better. And a lot less waste, so I do not need to hunt as often, good news for the rest of you.

Michael lived not far from me, in Hammersmith a bit west of Earl's

Court. I arrived about a quarter after two and seeing him after he buzzed me in, it was obvious that he was beside himself with excitement.

He grabbed my and pulled, "Come here, wait 'til you see this." To my surprise we stopped on the floor below his and knocked on a door, which was opened by an elderly woman who, upon seeing me, stepped back a little whispering, "My God. I can't believe it." I was now very curious since I consider myself neither handsome enough nor ugly enough to elicit gasps of disbelief.

"Mrs. Brenner, this is Sebastian. Sebastian, Mrs. Brenner." I bowed and she, having recovered her composure, extended a hand, a practice with which that I had not yet become comfortable. For centuries, a new or casual connection between persons of the opposite sex precluded anything as familiar as touching. I took her hand, but she had noticed.

"You are very old-fashioned, I suppose because you're Italian."

"Old habits are strongest."

"How old could they be in one so young?"

At which point Michael, who had been bouncing with impatience broke in. "Mrs. Brenner is a recent widow…"

Now I interrupted, inclining toward Mrs. Brenner, "My deepest sympathy."

"Thank you."

Michael began to talk, faster and louder than necessary, trying to make certain he was not interrupted again.
"

Mrs. Brenner married a German widower after the war. He had a son, Heinz, who had been killed in the war. "

The name Heinz Brenner struck a chord. He was one of the SS team. I was now becoming uneasy.

Michael was continuing, "Going through her husband's belongings, we found this photograph." Lifting a Manila envelope from a table, he took out a 10 x 8 photograph and handed it to me. "Look. Isn't that incredible." I looked and had to fight down an almost overwhelming urge to rip it to confetti. Taken from the left front, it showed four pall-bearers, three on the left—Erich, Heinz, and a man whose name I could not remember. The pallbearer on the right front was I. I took a deep breath, pretended not to notice and asked "Wh...Which is your step-son?" Turning it over I saw the inscription: *Heinz mit seine Freunde bei Volkers Beerdigung. München, 22-8-34* (Heinz with his friends at Volker's funeral). "Heinz."

"I...I don't know." She shrugged her shoulders, "I never saw it before this morning. Eduard never showed it to me. I thought he didn't have a picture of his son who was killed in the war."

Michael, consumed with his thought, was insensitive to Mrs. Brenner's discomfort at not being able to recognize her husband's son, took the picture and demanded, "Look here!" pointing to my picture, "Isn't that amazing?"

"What's amazing? Just a man in uniform."

"Can't you see? He looks exactly like you."

"It's difficult to determine with the hat." I resorted to mockery, "I suppose there is a superficial resemblance, two eyes, two ears, all other features present and accounted for."

"Oh, be serious. The resemblance is uncanny."

Mrs. Brenner was downcast, looking sad and uncomfortable but said nothing.

Michael was ploughing on, "The lads will have a laugh out of this."

"I do not want the 'lads' to have a laugh. I get enough of that for being Italian."

"What do you mean?"

"A barely concealed mixture of condescension and contempt. If you convince them that I am the reincarnation of a Storm Trooper I shall have to leave the country."

Michael got out a "But..." when Mrs. Brenner broke in, "You're right. Eduard faced the same thing."

Grateful for the opportunity to change the subject, I asked, "How did you and Mr. Brenner meet?"

"He was a very good mechanic and in the British Zone he was useful to an English major whose family had a machine business. When the major returned home in 1947, he sponsored Eduard and gave him a job, even though Edward was nearly sixty. I was a typist in the firm and we got on very well, both alone." She had a small smile at the memory.

Michael was not to be side-tracked. "You know, collectors pay for war memorabilia." Turning to Mrs. Brenner, "You might be able to get fifty quid for this since it's annotated and dated."

Mrs. Brenner seemed torn. "I don't know, though the money would be nice."

I saw my chance. "As a matter of fact, I am a collector. I will be happy to give you fifty pounds for the picture. The advantage of selling it to me is that another collector could track down the identities using the date in Munich. I am certain that Mr. Brenner would not want it known that Heinz was a Storm Trooper." My assumption that to keep the secret, she would forgo discovering which man was Heinz was correct.

Michael finally said something intelligent. "That works out very nicely for you," inclining toward Mrs. Brenner, and to me, "I suppose you won't be showing it around."

"A sagacious supposition."

Mrs. Brenner looked slightly surprised and said, "You speak excellent English for a foreigner." Condescension but not contempt.

I gave her the money. Later at home I burned it.

What did you think I would do? I am not sentimental nor can I afford to be.

If you are curious, no, I did not dine on Michael, however tempted I was upon seeing the picture and listening to him babble about showing it around.

HALF A BUBBLE
OFF PLUMB

1

New York in the 1970's probably resonates with you more than, say, Lübeck in the 1170's, so I favor more modern adventures in these reminiscences.

I had become much more sophisticated in the ways of modern finance. I set up mutual funds in tax havens where I could open accounts for my new identities and transfer money between names. I also chartered dummy companies that would rent my apartments and buy the dining rooms and the little companies that I use as a front for luring prey. Personal expenses, like clothes, are always paid cash. Other than my driver's license and passport I try to leave no records.

As implied, the 1970's found me living in New York for the first time since leaving Veronica, with an Australian identity I had acquired in Adelaide. New York will become one of the cities I regularly circulate through. I try to be in one place for about 10 years, roughly from ages 25 to 35. The cities I love —New York, Paris, London, Rome, get me about every 80 years with other large cities filling in—Chicago and Los Angeles in the United States, many others in Europe and Latin America.

After the theater one night, I was walking through Central Park to my apartment on the West Side. Not many people did and I was nearly alone. One would think it would be a prime feeding ground for me but I really need to get the meal to my dining room so I can properly drain and dispose of the body. A little more than halfway through, a young man approached. He was looking in all directions and seeing no one, pulled a pistol from his jacket pocket, told me to freeze and he came closer.

"Gimme your money!" I was obeying, reaching to my back pocket for my wallet when, through intent, nerves, or accident, the pistol went off. I fell to the sidewalk, face up. He bent over and reached to turn me over to get at my wallet. I grabbed him by the throat and his right wrist (the hand that held the pistol). His position left him unbalanced and I was able to flip him on his back. That, and the fright at having me come back to life caused him to drop the pistol and scream. Sitting on him, I picked up the pistol with one hand and put my other forearm over his mouth which muffled, but did not stop his screams. The terror in his eyes I had seen many times. While I did not have the hunger, and no particular desire to kill him, I cannot allow stories of a man who will not die spreading. I placed the muzzle of the pistol under his chin and fired. I tried to make it look like suicide, putting the pistol in his hand. I would have moved to body behind a bush, but the bullet had come out through the top of his head, leaving blood and brain on the sidewalk.

Such preparation was all for naught. The morning tabloids described a murder-robbery. A man was found in Central Park without a wallet and the police were looking for help in identifying him. No weapon was found.

I was not the only predator roaming the city.

2

During this stay in New York, I encountered what may have

been a masochist for the only time in my long existence. Or more precisely, the only one I believed to be masochistic. It started with a personal in one of the underground papers. I read these regularly because they often lead to lonely people who would provide a healthy repast. "Mid-twenties SM seeks adventurers for extreme pleasure. Sex and race not important. Lower Manhattan." I was not certain what was meant by "extreme pleasure", but it roused my curiosity which, unlike the proverbial cat, would not kill me. I briefly speculated whether SM meant single male or sadomasochist. There was a box number for reply, which I promptly sent using my Post Office box in Queens, suggesting we meet a week later at a fast food place near Washington Square, popular with NYU students, at six. It was November and would be dark. In a crowd, two more are not noticed and I never want to be identified with any of my prey. I said I would be wearing a Pittsburgh Pirates tee shirt. He sent a card with the word, "Yes" signed Barry.

I arrived half an hour early and had to wait a few minutes for a table to become free. Shortly thereafter, Barry introduced himself. He was younger than I expected, looking not even twenty. He looked about an inch shorter than I, about 5 feet 9. Taking off his jacket, he was wearing a slightly too small white tee shirt which showed that he worked out. He was cute rather than handsome with brown eyes and straight dark brown hair that hung over his forehead and rested on his ears. When he smiled he showed very white teeth.

"How did you get into this stuff?" he asked.

"What is 'this stuff?' Perhaps you should tell me what you want. What do you do with people now?"

"I don't do anything with anyone." He sounded and looked unhappy. "That's why put in the ad." He stopped not knowing how to put his fantasies into words.

"Well then, what have you been doing alone? Only dreaming

or do-it-yourself?"

"It's not enough to do it by myself. I want a friend." He looked at me with what I assumed was hope.

"Tell me about yourself, Barry. What do you do? I mean, are you a student or working?"

"I don't do anything. My parents were killed in an accident when their car was hit by a semi whose driver had fallen asleep and between their insurance and the settlement I don't have to do anything. I left my hick town upstate and now I want to live as I please. I can pay you."

"I do not need money. But you still have not told me what you want."

He looked around. "Can we find someplace private? I don't want people to hear. Beside, you might get angry and yell at me."

I smiled my sincerest false smile. "Don't worry, nothing, nothing you can say will surprise me or make me angry. The worst that can happen is for me to say no and we walk out together. No one is paying the least attention to us, they all have their own problems."

Barry moved closer and lowered his voice to almost a whisper. "For as long as I can remember, I've thought about stabbing myself at the climax of sex. But I'm not suicidal. I'd like to have a very painful experience at the climax of sex but not die. Or die but then come back...did you swallow the wrong way?"

"Yes. I'm okay. Go on, I'm really curious as to where this is going."

He gave a kind of laugh. "I don't really know myself." He stopped. "I've had a couple of girlfriends but they weren't what I wanted. One tied me up and beat me while jerking me off. Let's say she enjoyed it a lot more than I did. Another, during one of our sessions, squeezed my balls so hard I nearly fainted and she drew blood with her nails."

"Again, what do you want?"

He blinked and swallowed. "Oh, hell. I might as well say it. The problem is that I can't do everything myself: jerk off, play with my balls, use a dildo, pinch my nipples, and press a knife into my belly button."

"Why the knife?"

"The pain makes the orgasm so much better."

"Octopus have the right idea. You need more than two arms."

"Don't laugh at me."

"I'm not. I'm sympathizing. But it sounds as if you need three of four pairs of hands."

Again, he looked unhappy. I put my hand on his forearm and said, "You are treading on dangerous ground. Who knows what will come out of the sewer with that personal you placed? How many responses did you get, by the way?"

"More than I expected. You're the first I've met, because you chose a place like this. Others suggested lonely, out-of-the-way places or they would pick me up on some corner." A little smile. "I may be crazy, but I'm not stupid."

"Don't brag. What precautions are you taking? Even if I agreed, you have no way of knowing whether I'm homicidal or really sadistic. Conversely, how do I know that you would not be setting me up for torture and murder? What you want cannot be done in a public place like this."

"I've thought about that. What we do is each tell a friend where we're going and who we'll be with."

"Whom."

"Huh?"

"*Whom* we'll be with. Even better, with whom we'll be. Bad grammar bothers me."

"Oh." He looked dubious, wondering with what, or whom, he was dealing.

I resumed. "Do you just want me to help you with your enjoyment or do you expect to do unto me what you want done unto you?"

He brought his eyebrows down toward the bridge of his nose, looking quite skeptical. "You sure talk funny. I don't think you're taking me seriously."

"Believe me, I take you seriously. I really want this to come off. I just want to make certain that you do not have all the fun."

The eyebrows came back up and he was wide-eyed. He even smiled.

I continued, "Your idea about telling people is a good one. It protects us both in case one of us really is a madman." I laughed to show that the idea was absurd.

He sat up straight and smiling. "When can we start? Is tomorrow at my place too soon?"

He suggested early afternoon; I wanted after dark, pleading work. We exchanged addresses. He lived in the Village and I gave him my dining room in Queens, rented under another name which I also gave him. Now I just had to get Barry there.

That night I had to think out how I was going to handle this. I could not do anything at his apartment nor could I let him know that I had no sex life—one of the two things I would change about this body. The hunger was beginning and I was looking toward having Barry sooner rather than later. Unlike Barry, I find nothing sexy about pain and have never gotten used to it, though I have sometimes had to be philosophical about bearing it.

The next day, Wednesday, I went to Barry's apartment and he opened the door wearing a gray and black silk shirt with the top three buttons undone and jeans. He started to unbutton the shirt but I put my hand on his, "Let me." I worked slowly, touching his genitals, rubbing his torso, first with the shirt on and then as I unbuttoned it. I wish the women I had when I was Octavian had reacted the way Barry did. He was panting in anticipation and making noises that sounded very satisfied. When he was naked, I undressed, we complimented each other on our bodies. He asked, "Where do you work out?"

"The Y in Queens." I guessed that there must be a Y somewhere in Queens, and quickly added, "Since this is your party, you can go first. I shall start you off with a warm oil rubdown," picking up the bag I had brought, "and then we shall go from there."

We went into the bedroom, he lay on the bed and I knelt beside him. From the bottle, I poured the oil into a small carafe over a candle and while it warmed, Barry described what he wanted.

"I'll play with one nipple and press the knife in my belly-button. You take my cock and the other nipple. Make it as long as possible. Okay?"

"As I said, it's your party."

While talking and waiting for the oil to heat, I was brushing his erogenous areas very gently with my fingertips.

"Are you a fag? You touch like a girl."

"I'm trying to do to you what I like women to do to me."

"I can barely feel it. Don't rub, pinch. Hard."

I did and he went erect almost immediately, did our most libidinous young Barry.

The oil was ready and I had him turn over. I began the rubdown and within a minute or two he was rubbing his crotch up and down against the sheet. I slapped his buttocks and said playfully, "Stop that or you will shoot your load and miss the rest of the fun."

"I can come twice in an hour," with more than a touch of pride, but he stopped.

Turning over, we got to the main event. After coating him with the oil, I stroked him gently, bringing him almost to climax then easing off. Every time, he would push the knife a little harder until he finally drew blood. As I watched the blood fill up the cavity, I had to fight down a strong desire to push the knife all the way in and drink. Not convinced of his sanity, concerned he really would stab himself either purposely or in sexual frenzy, and not wanting to have to call an ambulance or leave a body where I might have been known to have been, I immediately brought him to climax. All the while he had been making groans of what I supposed was delirious pleasure. That reminded me of how much I had enjoyed sex and made me jealous.

"Wow! That was fantastic. Can we do it again?"

"Not tonight. I have to get home, early morning."

"Tomorrow?"

"Sorry, I have tickets to a play."

He calmed, a little. "What are you seeing?"

"*Butley*, with Alan Bates, at the Morosco." I gave enough details to convince him I indeed had tickets—which I did.

"The *Times* gave it a good review." I was surprised he read the

Times, snob that I am. "How about Friday?"

"Friday is fine, this time at my place. I have some very interesting gadgets."

"Can I try them?"

"Friday is my turn. I hope you were paying attention tonight."

"I was. But you don't work Saturday, do you? We can stay late, first you, then me."

"Oh, okay. About six. Hey, what you said about staying late gives me an idea. Why don't we have dinner? I enjoy cooking and my friends are kind enough to say I'm good at it."

"Great. I don't cook and I don't get a home-cooked dinner very often."

"Fish, flesh, or fowl?"

"I like fish, but I eat just about anything except chicken. My parents raised chickens and we had it almost every day."

The next morning I went up to Queens to put the name I had given Barry on the mail box and buzzer and prepared a spot in the cellar. That evening, dinner and *Butley* with acquaintances. I endured the dinner and enjoyed the play and company.

Friday afternoon I spent shopping. Because food is only texture without taste I have to follow recipes closely. "Season to taste" is meaningless to me. I had acquired a strong sedative that has no effect on me. I will put in a good word for corruption, it makes everything go more smoothly for those of us who must operate *sub rosa*.

Barry arrived a few minutes early and came into the kitchen while I finished cooking. We had filet of sole with a Dijon mustard velouté, which contained the sedative, carrots with butter and clove, and broccoli with butter. The mustard and cloves would conceal whatever taste the sedative might have.

I took a bottle of Pouilly-Fumé from the refrigerator. "Are you old enough to drink?"

"I'm 22."

"You don't look it."

He reached to his back pocket, "I can show you my driver's license."

"Never mind. We shall not drink that much anyway. Liquor would interfere with our performance."

Barry enjoyed the food. Until he lost consciousness, which he did quietly. Becoming unsteady, he dropped his fork and reaching over to retrieve it, tumbled off the chair and did not move. I put him on a heavy quilt and dragged him head first to the cellar, bumping him down the stairs.

After draining him, I buried him in the cellar and, since there was not time to hire someone to lay a floor, covered the grave with some old furniture. It was useless if the address were found but I thought it about fifty-fifty that Barry would not leave the information with someone. He had struck me as a feckless young man, one who would think that telling me what he was going to do would be enough to assure my good behavior. I removed the name from the mailbox on my way out.

Later, at my apartment, I wondered if I should have sent Barry off according to his fantasy—stabbing him at climax. The intense pain of being stabbed by Andrew was my most vivid memory of life. Would Barry have found the combination of pain and sex equal to his fantasy? Strange though it sounds, coming from one who has littered the centuries with the bodies of his prey, I hate seeing people in pain and, Volker Schmidt excepted, have never consciously inflicted it.

It appeared that Barry did not have many, or any, close

friends. It was almost a week before the newspapers mentioned he was missing and since he was a wealthy young man, kidnapping was feared. It was only because of a call from a trainer at his gym that the police made a wellness check. The next day it was reported that material was found in his apartment indicating that he may have engaged in dangerous activities. The activities were left to the reader's imagination. Persons with information were asked to contact the police. Two days later his car was found in a rough neighborhood of the Bronx, completely stripped. After more than forty years, I now take this opportunity to thank whoever stole his car and thoughtfully left it in an entirely different borough. The police suggested he had been carjacked and were concerned for his safety. Barry's wallet, which I destroyed, contained the slip of paper with the name and address I had given him and there was no mention that the police found a copy in his apartment. Soon, Barry faded from the news. Apparently he had not given anyone the information about where he would be. Part of me is always curious as to what would be made of a body drained of blood, but never curious enough give the police an anonymous call with the location.

Since no one came to the Queens house, I was able to use the cellar until I filled it and had a floor laid.

Three or four months later Barry was briefly back in the news. Relatives were asking that he be declared legally dead and, as he left no will, were fighting over his money.

IDENTITY THEFT

Long before the term became common I was engaged in identity theft. After all, I cannot continue using a passport showing I was born in 1891. The necessity of re-establishing myself every ten or twelve years forces me to begin looking for a new identity beginning a few years before the switchover. In centuries past it was fairly easy simply to move on with a new name. Until the twentieth century international communications were cumbersome and lengthy. As I moved about Europe there were no visa requirements or length of stay restrictions. I could come to New York from London and stay as long as I wanted without either government being concerned with my whereabouts or activities as long as I remained quiet and out of sight. Personal documentation was simple to forge or acquire.

Now the stringent requirements for proving one's provenance make the process much more demanding. In the twenty-first century it is increasingly difficult to change identities. Governments have greatly expanded regulations, surveillance and technological innovations to control the issuance of passports and other identity documents.

During the last one hundred years I have developed a method that is working well, for now. When I begin to plan a change of residence, I acquire a low skill small business through a dummy holding company which allows me to hire people for which, of course, I require a birth certificate and other necessary information such as, in the United States, a Social Security number. This time it was a courier service used for same day deliveries within greater Chicago. I hired late teens to early twenties—mostly high school and college students but for a new identity, I look for unattached runaways and drifters, young men who will not be missed. Turnover was rapid so friendships were not deeply formed.

Thus prepared, I can entice prey.

A large city always has rootless young men—runaways, hustlers, people looking for an opportunity or an escape from whatever they are leaving. I look for a young man, late teenager actually.

In 2005, I had been in Chicago for seven years as an Austrian. It was time to plan my next move. I began frequenting places where I could meet boys of about sixteen to nineteen. As always, I wanted someone without many ties to society, not so difficult these days. I won't bore you with my many failures but after several months I found such a boy, let's call him John since I do not want to make tracking him down too easy by using his real name which, in due time, became mine and we do not want to keep track of a lot of Sebastians. A damp, raw November afternoon and he was sitting on a wall at Loyola University.

"Sitting in class can't be worse than sitting out here."

"Oh, I'm not a student. I tried to go in but they won't let me in without an ID." He paused and looked embarrassed. "Could you please give me a couple of dollars for a hamburger?"

I handed him a five. "Are you interested in a job?"

"Thanks and yes. I've been looking but nobody will hire me because I'm homeless."

"How do they expect you to stop being homeless without a job?"

"That's what I wonder."

"Let's go get that hamburger and talk about a job." We walked to a nearby McDonald's.

He got a Big Mac, fries and a soda. Explaining that I had had lunch, I ordered only a coffee.

"Is there any reason that you cannot be bonded?" He did not know what bonding is so I had to be blunter. "Have you ever been arrested for more than speeding? You will trusted to deliver packages and bonding is insurance that you are honest. The bond company will investigate your past."

He had a problem with that. He did not want his family to know where he was. I assured him that this would not occur. I knew that because I faked the bonding process.

"I was caught smoking marijuana when I was 15 but was told if I remained out of trouble the record would be expunged when I turned 18, which was a few months ago."

"And did you?"

"Yes."

"That shouldn't be a problem then. You will need a certified birth certificate which you can get from the city you where were born. Or do you have a passport?"

"No, I've never needed one." Another impediment gone. I cannot get a passport that duplicates one already issued.

"The job is physical. You will be loading and unloading trucks. The packages are generally not too large, mostly just envelopes. Eventually you will be picking up and delivering packages. Do you have a driver's license?" Again yes.

I gave him a business card and told him to come between 8 and 10 the next morning. "Where do you sleep? Do you crash at a friend's?"

"I don't have any. I'm too ashamed of myself." Perfect. "I find someplace outside on nice nights and a doorway when it rains. It's getting harder with the cold."

"Where do you keep your things?"

"Everything I have is in my backpack."

"There's a cheap hotel not far from here. I'll show you. Here's an advance." I gave him $100 and we walked to the hotel. I did not go in with him.

Often that is the last I see of the person, but John showed up the next morning just after eight. After filling out the paper-work, including a bogus bond application (word processing makes really official looking documents), I turned him over to the Teresa, the office manager.

I now had his social security number and a lot of personal information. In less than a month, with help from a Chicago official—always easily purchased-- I also had a birth certificate. John had not been born in Chicago but the combination of money and a sob story about how badly he needed the job got what I needed. John turned out to be a hard worker, happy to be earning $10 an hour. He found room and board with an elderly couple in return for helping around the house and yard. He was going to get his GED and then go to college. He had had enough poverty to last a lifetime. I truly regretted it when he "disap-peared" but necessity has no room for sentiment.

With all of the necessary documentation, I could now open an account in one of the banks I use, buying mutual funds and generally getting ready to assume my existence as yet another Sebastian. All of this takes between two and three years.

This time I had only about a year-and-a-half. In August, 2007 John asked if I could help him with an application for a passport. Since I had already obtained one in his name I had to act quickly.

"Where are you going?"

"The Stepanics are going to Croatia and want me to come to help."

"Sure, we can set aside some time tomorrow. In the morning I will pick up the forms and we can fill them out after lunch and then get the photos."

"Great. Thanks."

I then put together his morning run from the overnight deliveries—less expensive than same day—including one to my dining room. That night I prepared the house, not much work because I always try to keep one grave open. Also, prepare a story which by this time came easily.

At quarter past ten the next morning John came to the house on his scooter. My answering the door to his ring surprised him.

"What are you doing here?"

"Come in." He did. "I'm checking out this property for a client. Her company bought it a few weeks ago and she wanted my thoughts on rehabbing, but it seems to be in good condition. Why are you here?"

I have to deliver this." He held out a manila envelope. "Didn't you notice the address when you sorted?"

"I didn't think that she was using this address yet so I may have missed it or Teresa might have put your route together." I took the envelope and continued, "Now that you are here, I could use some help downstairs. How does your schedule look? It will take only a few minutes but the deliveries come first."

"I only have three more stops so I can help for a while and still get finished by noon."

I opened the door to the basement, turned on the light and motioned him to go ahead.

As he walked down I took a snub-nose .32 revolver from my jacket pocket and fired one bullet into the back of his head. Thus, instantly, from life to…what? I wish I knew. And so do you.

Leaving him as he fell, I went back outside to retrieve his scooter. It was parked on the walkway in front of the stairs. I had had a screen of hedges planted along the sidewalk with a solid gate which I now closed. The sides and back of the lot had a stockade fence. I value privacy. What I did not have was a garage or shed so I had to bring the scooter into the house. It was too heavy to lift or even drag up the stairs but I was able to lift the front wheel up one step and then the back until, four steps later, I had it on the stoop.

I had already picked up the passport forms so I returned to the office. A little after two I asked Teresa if John had returned.

"No," she checked his schedule, "and he should be done by now. It's not like him to be late."

"Perhaps he went home to change for the passport pictures."

She laughed, "Oh, men are so vain."

By four Teresa was sufficiently concerned to call John's house and was told they had not heard from him since he left in the morning. She turned to me, "I think we should check with the police to see if he's been in an accident." A divorced woman in her early forties with black hair and dark, almost black eyes, Teresa took a maternal interest in the young men and women we employed. I knew she would fret about John so I said, "Yes. I am worried myself." She called, describing John and the scooter, giving the license. Some twenty minutes later the police called back to say there were no reports of accidents involving motor scooters.

After work I went back, buried John and the scooter. I returned to my apartment in a three-flat in Andersonville a little after two AM.

When I opened the office about seven there was a message on the answering machine from Mrs. Stepanic, John's landlady. She sounded about to cry and asked us to call her as soon as we opened. I did. She and her husband were genuinely worried about John and were generous with their praise. The woman began sobbing at the thought that something bad may have happened to him. I told them I would file a missing person report and for them to expect a call from the police.

The police were inclined to think that John had, like many rootless persons, just taken off, stealing the scooter. They finally consented to send someone to get John's schedule (without, of course, the dining room). She did determine John's sequence of deliveries and the point when they stopped. After three days, she said they had come to a dead end and did we want to file a stolen vehicle report on the scooter. No.

The next year I sold I sold the business for a small profit. It had served its purpose and I do not like to work. In 2009, having refinished the cellar to put in a bedroom and bath, I sold the house, losing most of the profit from the business because of the housing market slump.

For the first time since the Civil War, I returned to Boston.

ENVOI

That brings us up to date. I am soon to assume my hundred and something identity, I cannot remember how many, and move on yet again. When I first discovered I was immortal and believed that my existence may have some purpose in God's plan, I thought it was all a very exciting adventure and was eager to learn how it would all turn out. That excitement long ago vanished. I try to fathom why God allows me to go on, killing ten to fifteen humans every year. Perhaps I am just another predator like a tiger or eagle, though not so magnificent, and in God's eye humans are held no higher than rabbits and field mice.

I have thought of one way to live more or less legally. I could have a blood center and buy blood from those willing to sell a pint. No doubt you have also thought of that. Even if the authorities allowed it, I doubt very strongly that people would accept "your friendly neighborhood vampire" and would agitate to have me move away. Drawing upon my long experience with humans I am certain that there would be no end of those testing my immortality—you kill one another with wanton abandon, and as a being widely perceived as a monster, I will be fair game to many. So I shall try to go on as I always have.

Emotionally, it is a lonely existence. I cannot have friends, someone in whom I can confide but who would be close enough to try to find me when I leave. You saw how complicated it got when I had to leave Veronica. I may not be the only one of my kind but I have no way of finding another. I cannot very well run a personal "Lonely vampire seeks same for companionship."

I can imagine a couple of my acquaintances meeting and the conversation going something like:

"Have you seen Sebastian recently?"

"No. Is he gone?"

"I guess so. I haven't seen him in a few months."

"Oh. Anyway, what do you think of the Red Sox' chances this year?"

I still do not know how or why I am what I am. Occasionally, I think that one of the voices from so long ago will finally say. "Oh, all right. I shall take him." and I shall keel over. Do they remember me? Do they care? Do they still exist? As always, questions without answers.

Technology may be closing in on me. Things like retinal scans or even the ubiquity of cameras frighten me. Where is my image? I am careful to remain anonymous and "off the grid" as the saying has it, but occasionally I imagine that in 2121 a robot security guard will pick up something about me that it can connect to 2021. Then what? That fear is not far-fetched. Security cameras are spreading their presence indoors and out. In a few years it will be nearly impossible to avoid them.

I may have to settle somewhere, not able to get a passport or driver's license.

How does it end? If I am captured and dropped into a hole of wet concrete to be trapped for eternity with only the hunger. Or cremated. If my body is reduced to nothing, will the hunger persist? Again I think back to the intermezzo. Will consciousness without substance have the hunger?

Except for that intermezzo between Octavian and Sebastian, I have had no evidence that anyone or anything takes the slightest interest in my existence, or the lives of the rest of you for that matter. Do they, whatever they were, still exist or were they simply one of an infinite cycles of the universe? Yet they set me on this path, bringing death to thousands.

If I were any kind of a man I would be racked with guilt and remorse.

But...

I am not...

Any kind of a man.

God is the only excuse I have and a thousand years ago I shouted, "What have You made me?" No answer came, then or ever. I do not know *what* God made me or *why*, but I *am* what God made me.

Thrown out of both and Hell, what do you do? There are no schools for vampires, you are on your own. Octavian, Prince of Rome at 17 and Pope John XII at 18--a priest and Pope only because his father wanted to ensure the family's hold on Rome and the Papal State. Young and libidinous, he uses his position for personal pleasures not at all befitting his office while struggling to keep those lands independent of powerful and greedy enemies. Murdered in his mistress's bed, his adventures and trials were just beginning as he wandered blindly learning to cope with the advantages, peculiarities and costs of his "afterlife."

Witness to wars and revolutions, great social changes and the small events that make up day-to-day life, this is his story as remembered and told by himself.

ABOUT THE AUTHOR

David Herder

Ever since seeing Bela Lugosi in Dracula some 65 years ago, I have wondered why and how a vampire becomes a vampire and how he or she goes about learning to be a vampire. This book attempts to answer those questions.